THE HAPPY ACCIDENTS
OF SILVA JONES

Dawn Vincent

Disclaimer: For the purposes of this novel, the conception of Rose was an accident. It is not legally possible to consent to sex while drunk, but I thank you for the suspense of disbelief for your enjoyment of the novel and I hope that the content is not upsetting for anyone.

*Is it weird to dedicate a novel to a cat? Well, if it is, never mind.
This is for Abbi, who was very much in the way throughout
the writing of so much of this novel in its earlier forms.
She reminded me to take a break to cuddle her, and get up
sometimes, as she never missed a chance to snack. She also
taught me to type one-handed while she used the other as a
dribble pillow. I miss you, fuzzball.*

*This book is also for all of us who have found the
deepest joys of our lives were in the accidental
and the unexpected turns it took.*

CHAPTER 1

Silva was not feeling brilliant as she tried and failed to tame her wild curls. The night before, they had behaved themselves when teased into soft ringlets that cascaded down her neck. The hairspray and the sweat of last night's dancing made her look like she had been experimenting with the fuse box. She managed to wrangle it into a high ponytail and ignored the crunchy feeling when she smoothed it over.

'You are not seriously going out like that are you?' her best friend, Layla asked as Silva wriggled her toes into her flip-flops.

'It's only the corner shop. I need something to feel less sick.'

'A shower would be a good start,' Layla said with raised eyebrows, 'you stink of cigarettes and B.O. and the worst bit is, my bed does too.'

'Sorry about that. I don't remember how I got home or why I ended up in your room,' Silva blushed.

'It's fine,' Layla said and smiled, 'you came home with Jake and I – he crashed on the sofa and left really early. I went to the loo and got us a glass of water and when I came back you had faceplanted my bed. I imagine you were looking for me. It was quite sweet actually. You were hugging my cushions.'

'I'll wash your bedding when I can handle that much movement at once.'

'How about this – I'll do the bed if you get us both plenty of goodies down the shop, seeing as you are dressed and appear to have no shame about going there looking as you do. You could meet your Prince Charming, but you'd never know as he would just think you were homeless and eating out of bins.'

'If I say "deal" and also promise to shower upon return, will you stop going on about it?' Silva asked, her stomach churning. When Layla agreed to those terms, Silva opened the door and gingerly took the staircase down to the bottom floor.

Upon her return, Silva laid out her haul of crisps, sugary drinks and chocolate. She sipped a can of energy drink, feeling a bit better despite knowing full well how terrifyingly bad the drinks were for her.

'Nice choices.' Layla said, pulling open a bag of salted crisps.

'And absolutely no possible men bumped into, so on this occasion, you are wrong.' Silva laughed.

There were a few minutes of quiet while they ate and Layla channel-hopped.

'So, Silv. What happened to you last night?' Layla asked.

Silva smoothed her crisp packet down and folded it into a triangle. A wave of nausea came over her and she pulled a blanket over herself and took another sip of her drink as she remembered the night before.

She and Layla had sung at the top of their lungs as they jostled for mirror space. They both laughed as they inevitably collided, but Silva simply grabbed Layla and they danced together.

'Is this why girls take so long to get ready?' Jake had asked as he let himself into the flat, helped himself to a cold beer bottle from their fridge, and had a smile on his face as he walked into the girls' living room to find them in vest tops and pyjama shorts.

'At least we're making an effort!' Layla said and laughed, breaking free from Silva and hugging Jake hello, then reaching into his hairline to play with the gelled spikes affectionately. He grinned at Layla, who released him and went into the kitchen for more drinks.

'This doesn't look like "a quiet drink" to me,' Jake said, smiling his winning smile.

'No, but I – we – fancied looking nice. We haven't been out

in *ages*. I've not had a night out in... I can't even remember.' Silva said.

'Are you sure it isn't just memory loss from Sambuca?'

'Quiet. The night is all mine. Ours. We are all celebrating. Let's enjoy it – and I don't care that it's a couple of G&Ts and maybe a curry. I bought this dress. I love it. It wants to enjoy itself.' Silva laughed, picking up her sequinned minidress and shaking it, almost blinding Jake as it caught the light.

'You'll look like a disco ball.'

'That, my friend, is my intention.' Silva said and grinned, taking her drink from Layla. The word "friend" had slipped out by accident and it stung her to say it.

Jake took himself to the kitchen and decided to make something for them all; he wasn't convinced they would actually make it anywhere for dinner. He smiled fondly at their abysmal ingredients but found something to make while they finished getting ready.

In the living room, Silva shimmied her way into her petrolescent sequins, enjoying the gentle rustle with every movement.

'You sound a bit like Santa as he flies through the night sky.' Layla said.

'Are you saying that I am fat and beardy?'

'NO! Although you HAVE done your moustache, haven't you?' Layla said, pretending to check as Silva threw a cushion at her. She smiled, happy to have avoided putting her foot in her mouth with a comment about Silva's body; she was concerned and had tried to get her to eat a bit more, but Silva just wasn't interested.

'Guys, I've made something – we should really eat something now, if we're having some drinks first, we won't eat for a while... I sound like my mum...but look what I made!' Jake said, bringing in a plate of appetizers he was quite proud of.

'You made that...from our fridge contents?' Layla asked in disbelief.

'I know! I rescued a mushroom, a little bit of spinach that

3

was on the turn, cheese, and crackers…and pesto. Honestly, try one.'

They were four glasses into a potent mixture of improvised cocktails, but both could tell the food was good. Between them, they finished the plate within a minute.

They finished getting ready, Layla in her skin-tight jeans, glittery boots, and crop-top, Silva in her tiny dress and black heels (which Jake eyed and Silva insisted were comfortable but if she was drunk enough, wouldn't stop him holding her up as she hobbled home), and Jake in his gelled hair, ironed jeans, white top, and leather jacket. He looked like a member of a 90's boy-band, but it suited him, so the girls didn't interfere.

An hour and a half later, they had not reached anywhere resembling somewhere they could have a quiet drink, and were certainly unlikely to be having a curry. Silva was on a stage in a nightclub, drunkenly shouting her best wishes to her friends into the mic that was set up for the band that had already played.

'EVERYONE! This is JAKE, he just got an AMAZING promotion and he's going to work in NEW YORK! We are really proud but we will miss him,' she slurred. 'AND THIS IS LAYLA, SHE IS GOING TO BE RUNNING THE NEW COFFEE LOUNGE IN TOWN!' Silva told the room happily. Most of that was drowned out by the thump of the bass through the speakers. The DJ looked irritated. Layla ran up to the stage and Jake breathed a sigh of relief; she would put a stop to this, he thought.

'AND THIS IS SILVA, SHE HAS AN INTERIOR DESIGN COMPANY THAT'S ABOUT TO LAUNCH!' Layla yelled and Jake didn't know what to do with himself, so he closed his eyes, laughed, and made a move to get up to stop them, not wanting to leave their drinks unattended but if needs must…

Luckily, the owner of this particular club walked up to Silva and Layla, smirking, his eyebrows raised.

'I thought I told you two you weren't welcome after the last time!' he shouted.

'You shouldn't have cheap cocktails on then!' Silva laughed and so did he, although he slightly regretted his pricing at that precise moment in time.

'Fair point. Right. You can have a free round if you get away from the mic and go somewhere else after!' he said, keen to keep the rest of the clientele happy.

'DEAL!' Layla yelled, Silva just smiled and started dancing on the spot. Layla hauled Silva to the bar to collect on the drinks before he could change his mind.

They left shortly afterwards, now swimming in enough alcohol to want to dance more. Silva hobbled a little on her heels as they stepped out, Jake automatically giving her an elbow to lean on. Silva shrugged him off.

'They're comfortable!' she protested. Jake caught Layla's eye. She rolled hers, he just shook his head.

They had found another nightclub and danced, having taken full advantage of potent shots on trays held by bored girls with contactless card readers, so they were now a level of drunk that had started to become hazy and the events from then on blurred in Silva's mind, but she remembered finding someone attractive and pulling them into a toilet cubicle, her dress shaking like a rainmaker as she kissed and was kissed.

Back in their front room with Layla staring at her, Silva flushed.

'There was a guy.' she said.

'I knew it.' Layla laughed. 'I've been trying to work out if that's a bruise on your neck or a love bite.'

Silva flushed, having completely missed that in the mirror. She touched her cool hand to where Layla was looking and it was tender.

'And what else did you do with this guy?' Layla asked, smirking.

Silva recalled the clumsy fumbling of hands as they undid zips and lowered knickers, the bass so hard it made the walls vibrate but not loudly enough to cover up the sound of someone being violently sick in the next cubicle. For reasons that make sense only to very drunk, very horny people, that didn't put them off.

'Is this real?' Silva had whispered, at the level of drunk where she wasn't quite sure where she was but absolutely into what she was doing. His reply was muffled under kisses, but it didn't seem to matter. She was lost in the moment. A groan and some giggles broke it and the short-but-sweet encounter was over.

'You go out first,' Silva slurred, leaning heavily on the cubicle door when her legs failed to co-operate.

'But it's full of girls,' the male said.

'Wimp,' Silva replied simply, laughing, not focusing. There was a flush and then a slam that shook the cubicle wall and she grabbed the door for stability. The taps ran, the door opened and closed, and then there was silence.

'Um, I should go while it's empty in here.' the male said, slurring his words.

'Run for it.' Silva replied, not as quietly as she thought she had.

She listened for the tack-tack of his trainers on the sticky floor and clicked the door open when the coast was clear.

Silva looked at Layla, who was waiting for an answer back in the present moment. 'A very messy fumble in the toilets – pretty sure we had sex.'

Layla laughed. 'Were you safe?' she asked.

'Of course,' Silva lied. She had no memory either way. She sniffed her wrist on impulse; remembering something.

The coast had not been clear when she had left the cubicle. A woman was sat on a chair by the sink, staring at her, having heard everything. She hauled herself up and spritzed Silva with perfume and held out her hand. Silva popped a couple of sweaty pound coins in her waiting palm, wondering idly if she smelt bad enough to need the assault on her senses that she had just endured, and paid for. She remembered looking in the mirror next. Staring back at her was a very drunk woman who looked pretty in an unkempt way: wild ginger curls, blue eyes, flushed cheeks and a love bite bruise forming on her neck.

'Any idea who it was?' Layla asked, and Silva shook herself

from the appended memory.

'Nope. Not a clue, Layla. Then I left the bathroom, found you and you suggested calling it a night and getting food.'

'Yes, you looked *very* happy with that idea. And I knew it was time because you were drunk enough to let yourself be attacked by the perfume bottle lady.'

Silva nodded. 'I think I'm going to go for that shower. See if I can wash some of the shame off me.'

'Scrub especially hard just for the perfume. It's like glitter – it won't leave you until it decides to.' Layla smirked.

Silva rolled her eyes and got up gingerly, her stomach churning and her head hurting. She went to the kitchen and filled the last clean mug with water, shaking her head and smiling at the mountain of washing up that Jake had added to. She played out the last few flashes of the evening in her head like stills from a movie as she peeled her pyjamas off and stepped into the shower.

They had found Jake dancing with a group of girls, in the centre of the dancefloor, looking happy but tired. At the suggestion of food, he nodded like a happy toddler and they walked arm-in-arm with Silva in the middle to get her to walk in a straight line in her evil shoes. The still-warm summer air made them feel as though the whole world was beautiful, anything was possible and their lives were where they wanted them to be. They ate on a kerbside, refusing to sit down in the chippy for some reason, despite having entertained the employees with their singing, then somehow hobbled a mile home, with no recollection of how or how long it took them.

Little did Silva know, as the heat of the water made her feel better and worse at the same time, that this was only the beginning of her hangover.

CHAPTER 2

Six weeks later, Silva woke with a start and instantly knew that she was going to vomit, and she had maybe ten seconds before it happened. She launched herself out of bed as quickly as she could, then ran to the toilet, remaining there afterwards, a cold sweat beading on her forehead. She waited a few minutes, then got up gingerly and edged her way to the kitchen to scavenge something to make her feel better, found a can of cheap cola and hoped it would help settle her stomach.

She sat on the sofa and pulled a blanket over herself, trying to warm up her limbs; she was rather cold and it was only the end of September; the full force of autumn hadn't crept in yet.

Letting a bit of cola go down, she tried some more but it seemed it was too much; once again she got up and ran to the toilet and vomited.

'No, no, no,' she whispered, trying not to wake Layla up on her only day off. 'I cannot be ill. I have a client. Please just hold off until tomorrow. Please.'

She thought hard about what it could be. She hadn't eaten anything questionable that she could think of, hadn't been drinking the night before- or the night before that, even, as hangovers sometimes liked to last two days or delay a day to make her think she was safe.

Layla knocked gently on the door.

'Silv, everything okay?'

Silva groaned in response. Layla pushed open the door and gasped. 'You're really pale. Have you been sick? Whatever it is, I don't want it. Are you okay? I'll make us some food…'

At the mention of food, Silva's stomach turned again and she turned back to the toilet to give the very little amount of fluid she had left to it. Layla walked to her and put the back of her hand on Silva's forehead. 'You're not burning up or anything... what's going on? You've not been out drinking; we haven't eaten anything dodgy... no virus doing the rounds...unless you're patient zero.... oooh, you're not pregnant, are you?' Layla joked.

'Ha, ha.' Silva said with a withering stare. Layla shrugged and started running a bath with some of her endless supplies of oils and ointments to make Silva feel better. 'You don't really want a bath while I'm in here chundering do you?' Silva asked.

'It's for you, you idiot. If I picked nothing else up from my mother, it's how to make a bath into a magic potion.'
Silva didn't argue for a change, feeling too poorly to do much but agree to get in on the condition she could have a bucket in easy reach for sick.
Layla left her to it; checking she hadn't passed out and drowned every now and then while Silva lay in the bath until it went cold, enjoying the smells but something Layla had said had her immobilised.
Could it be morning sickness?
Well, could it?
Silva thought carefully. She had been working a lot for a long time, she hadn't had a boyfriend since the start of the year. She had only had the odd one-night stand but always used protection, she made sure of it, but she had run out of her pill and not bothered to replace it for a couple of months now, not seeing the point of it if she was happily single...
But then, there had been that night out. That guy...
She tried to draw from her memory the sound of a condom packet, or seeing him put one on, but came up blank. She definitely hadn't taken the morning-after pill; after all, she had been drunk, they had done something but it was messy, she hadn't even thought about the fact she might have...

'Oh, fuck, I've been stupid.' Silva groaned to herself as more and more little pieces of her puzzle clicked into place.

'Everything okay?' Layla called, popping her head round

the corner of the door, then changing her mind and coming inside to go for a wee.

'La-la, you know what you said about me being pregnant?' Silva asked.

Layla paused, the colour draining from her face. 'Yes?'

'I think I might be. Can you get me a pregnancy test? Please? And also, chocolate. Lots of it.'

Layla took a moment for that to sink in as she got off the toilet and washed her hands.

'Okay. Okay. I can do that – we need some food anyway. I mean, technically it's your turn to get food in but I'll let you off. Erm, sorry, babbling. Silv – I was joking? What? How? Who?'

'Let's not worry about that just yet – and I'm sure I don't need to explain *how* to you...' Silva said, grinning despite inner terror flashing in strobe lights.

Layla chuckled in response and nodded. 'Okay, hop out and I'll get showered and go.' she said.

*

Later, when Layla had returned and Silva felt a bit more human and had managed to keep down some tea and toast, they sat together waiting for the pregnancy test to line up with Silva's fate. Layla held her hand.

'Come on then, it should be done by now.' She said gently to Silva.

Silva picked it up with shaking hands and tears rolled down her face. She hadn't been sure of what to expect or how she would react and if she was honest, she still wasn't. Layla took the test from her.

'Oh, Silv.' She pulled her friend in for a tight hug, unsure whether this was a situation for "oh, shit" or "yay". She was guessing the former, but how could she be sure?

'Shall we do the other one to make sure? They can be wrong sometimes, can't they?' Silva asked. Layla shrugged; she had bought a multipack by accident.

Silva downed some water. Half an hour later, the next plastic stick came to the same conclusion.

'So...' Layla said, hoping to start a conversation. Silva was far too quiet.

'Shit.' Silva said, sitting back down on the sofa after pacing the room.

'I hate to have to ask you, Silv. But I'm going to. Two things: whose is it, and how do you feel about it?'

'I feel...terrified, Lay, like my whole life and everything I've ever worked for just caved in, like I have no idea if I want this, but I'm not 100% sure that I don't, that AGHHH OH MY GOODNESS and WHY ME and also... Layla, I have no idea whose it is. Not in an "I've slept with so many people, it's like my vagina has set me up for a game of Guess Who" way, no. I had sex with some randomer in the toilets at the club we went to a few weeks ago? You remember? You found me just after?'

'I did, you stank of teenage regrets thanks to that perfume-touting attendant. I didn't see anyone with you though.'

'I didn't fuck Casper the Friendly Ghost, Lay.' Silva said, then had to laugh at herself when Layla let out a snort. 'He left before me, I waited a few minutes to check I was alone – because you know, I'm subtle and demure-' she laughed again, '-and then got conned into paying a few quid to smell like a twit.'

'Silv,' Layla said carefully, collecting her thoughts. 'You were very drunk. Did he...did he make you do anything?'

'Lay, I *was* very drunk but so was he. I led him to those toilets. I know why you're worried, but it's okay. 100% consent. Fully responsible for feeding the urge of the person who took my fancy, and fine with it. I've got a feeling people are going to try to shame me for this, Lay. But why should I feel ashamed? If I keep the baby, of course, I'll have to tell people how she came about... but why should I be ashamed for something that men are celebrated for? That they slap each other on the back for? Fuck that. And if anyone wants to judge me for that then screw 'em.'

Layla smiled and nodded her agreement. 'Too right. Now, did I just catch you calling that little two-blue-liner "she"?'

Silva flushed and realised she had. She sighed and grabbed a bag of chocolate and tore it open. Layla couldn't stop her eyes widening at the sight of Silva eating something sugary and not being drunk or hungover at the time. That was her pattern; she would eat barely a thing most of the time, and the times she did eat a lot, she would go out and dance it all off in nightclubs with Layla. Being busy with careers and life had meant far fewer nights out, which had made Silva smaller and smaller, and in Layla's opinion she was starting to look unhealthy, so she took a very small amount of chocolate when offered and made sure Silva ate plenty.

'Okay. Let's get this thing hashed out. I know it's new. You have time to think about it; you're only about six weeks, aren't you? But best to talk it through while it's raw maybe?' Layla prompted.

'Yeah, true. My head is swimming, Layla. So is something in my uterus - which is terrifying. I guess my main concern is how I would do it? Scared that I just left my job to start a business; what the hell do I do with that?'

'Ask for your job back before it's obvious why, is what I would do if you don't think the business can cope, babes. Eric will understand.'

Silva nodded and chewed her lip then said, 'it just feels like a step back, that's all. And I can't help seeing you and Jake doing so well, and feeling like I'll just be "mum" and all my dreams will be finished and of course that's not a bad thing if I can bring up a child and love her and all of that but...I've worked so hard for so, so long.' She was crying now, her body juddering. The guilt she felt toward her business partner, Eric, suddenly hit her.

'Hey, hey. We share our lives with you but our lives aren't yours. Don't compare yourself to anyone else, Silv. Your life has just taken a bit of a fork – if you will pardon the pun – before ours have. You never know – Jake might come back from New York preggers too,' Layla said, chuckling.

Silva shook her head, laughing.

'I honestly think you'll be okay, Silv. You can do both things. You know you're good at this, you know you can earn enough to get by – and your identity can be many things. Take it from the girl who ran away from a forced marriage and into a life of - hopefully – happy business owner, adventurer, lady lover et cetera. You get to choose which parts of the identity you keep. Even if in some cases you have to change your name and go into witness protection but HEY never mind. I'm on a tangent. The point is: none of this was in my plan at one point. Life changed, so did I. I can't tell you from experience what having a great mother is like, but I know you'll be one, and a great interior designer, and that you'll be okay. You know who you are, Silv. That's brilliant. And I will help you where I can.'

'Thank you.' Silva said, mulling it over.

'You're welcome. You are going to be okay no matter what you decide to do. And whichever appointment you decide to book, you have my full support.'

Silva smiled, the support touching her heart. She closed her eyes and drew a deep breath. Layla was right, there was no need to make a decision right now, but she sort of already had. It terrified her to her core, but she was having a baby, and for some reason, had a feeling the baby was a girl.

'How will I do it alone?' Silva asked.

'Same way millions of women do. You're strong, and if you don't have a choice then you get on with it. Plus… you are the most stubborn person I've ever met in my whole life, Silv. It is possibly for the best – you know what you want to do, you can do it, you won't have anyone trying to stop you – just think, you could be with the father, and now bound to them for life. This is literally the perfect situation for you, in some ways.' Layla shrugged.

'That could have happened to me at 16, you know. I've been pregnant before,'

'Oh?'

'I was sixteen. I went out with this useless kid called Joe and we weren't as careful as we could've been.' Silva remembered the panic after she had told him, sat up in the long-abandoned ruins of a church.

He'd guessed something was up; she was unusually quiet

and they usually took those private moments to have sex.

She'd watched the fields through the doorway as she waited for a reaction. She couldn't look at his face. Birds shot up in the air as though they were crumbs on a bed sheet that had been shaken out. Slowly, they drifted down like leaves of confetti, defeated.

'You can't be,' Joe had choked out, his ginger hair standing on end.

'I am, Joe.' Silva had sighed.

'What are you going to do?'

That word had stung. *You.* As if it was only *her* fault.

'I was hoping you'd help me out with that one, you know, as it's your problem too,'

'I can't look after a baby, Silv,'

'You can't look after cress,'

'I know,'

'I don't want this baby,'

'You think I do?'

'Good. We're sorted then,'

He had taken his hand away so subtly she hadn't even noticed it.

'Well, to make this go away I'm going to need to get an abortion, Joe. My family cannot know about this. Can you help? With train fares and stuff for the hospital?'

'I don't know. Let me see if I can borrow some money from someone.'

She had smiled gratefully, aching inside and vowing she'd never be this dependent upon anybody ever again, even though she was only just sixteen.

'As it turned out, I didn't need his money. I bled our accident into the shower two days later. The poor mite wanted to get out before we could evict it. Which was just as well; that boy was about as helpful as head lice. Still, you always wonder, don't you? What would that life have been like?'

'Must have been tough,' Layla said, eyes wide, wondering how she had never heard this story before.

'I didn't have time to feel anything except relief, then I dumped him. He was so cold about the whole thing. He was the drummer in our band, so it kind of messed up his musical career. He's a lawyer now,' Silva said, still in memory lane.

She'd dumped Joe and then rejected Jake, his affections coming too soon after she'd had to cope with too much, too young. Her father died the week after she lost the baby and what she had thought was a solid boyfriend.

Silva regretted that now. Jake made her stomach prickle with nerves when she thought of him. It had only been six weeks but they had barely heard from him. Silva sighed again; a life with Jake was out of bounds now. She had a baby coming. If she wanted a relationship, it would have to be with someone sturdy, and who didn't polarise his internal magnets every time another girl walked past him.

Layla looked at Silva, a new understanding in her eyes. 'You don't know how strong you are, do you?' she asked. 'You are going to be fine, babes. Believe it of yourself. Now, go get ready. You have a client, haven't you?'

Silva nodded and got up as she realised she only had half an hour to get out of the door, and started rushing, happy to have the distraction despite her stomach still feeling like it was on a fast-spin cycle on a washing machine.

As she drove to her client, she did what you were supposed to do; she listened to her heart.

Unfortunately, all she could make out in its panicked rapid beats was this:

"*What will you do? What will you do? What will you do?*"

CHAPTER 3

Silva went to see her old boss the next afternoon with a sinking feeling in the pit of her stomach, as though the tiny embryo in there was pretending to be an anchor to match how she felt. It felt strange to not be alone in her own body now she knew about it, but mostly she was grateful that the sickness was confined to the morning.

She fluffed her fingers through her hair in the bathroom mirror, fiddled with her blouse to puff it out a bit and hide the new little swell to her stomach, and gave herself a shaky smile in the mirror.

'You've got this.' She whispered to herself as she left.

'What can I do for you, Silva?' Simi, her old boss asked, as they sat down.

Silva took a deep breath, hating having to do this. She had left on good terms; had liked her job well enough but was making enough from designing to go part-time and then, not needing it at all.

'Thank you for agreeing to meet me. I was wondering if you had any positions still available anywhere...I know I just left, but...' Silva felt her neck go red. 'I enjoyed this job, and I know what I'm doing. Unfortunately, my financial situation has changed and I need to work a job again, and you know I'm good at what I do, so if you need someone, I'm here, available to start as soon as possible.' She said, and smiled at Simi, thinking *please, please, please.*

'Silva...you were a fantastic employee. I'm sorry to hear about your situation, I really am...however your position has been filled, and due to cutbacks and the current climate...we aren't taking anyone else on at the moment, I'm truly sorry. I might be able to offer you ad-hoc things, freelance, you know, but other than that...'

Silva's heart plummeted to hang out with the embryo in her stomach. She was too proud to beg.

'Okay, Simi. Please stay in touch if something does come up. How are things here?'

'They're all good, thank you, Silva. Running as usual, really.' Simi smiled at her kindly. 'How are things with you?'

Silva winced, unable to share the only bit of news she had because it would hurt her chances of any work from Simi. It shouldn't, but it would.

'Okay thank you. Just a bit quiet on the bookings front, is all. But really enjoying the work I do get.'

'That's great. Well, feel free to go say hello to everyone. You will have to please excuse me, I have a conference call shortly that I need to prepare for. It was good to see you, Silva.' Simi said as she stood up. Silva accepted the dismissal but didn't go into her old office. She waited for Simi to go to the toilets, then left the building, teeth chattering despite there being no cold.

While she was still in formal clothes and had a few hours until she had her next client to speak to, Silva popped into the nightclub where she had gotten pregnant on the off-chance someone would be there; by day it was a dingy sports bar that was often open late afternoon.

A roar of football fans greeted her at the door; she was lucky, then. Hoping her smart attire made her look official, she went inside and walked up to the bar. The server, a lad of about 19, raised his eyebrows at her in bored confusion.

'How can I help?' he asked her.

'Hi, I'm – um – I have an unusual question,' Silva said, flustered, ruining the professional plan she'd had. 'I was in here about six weeks ago, and I lost something. Is there any way I could look at the CCTV? I think it was right at the entrance to the ladies' loos.'

The lad moved his chewing gum to the other side of his mouth.

'That would be in lost property, madam. Which is empty; we cleared it out the other day but nothing in there was of value that hadn't already been claimed.'

'Ah, right, ok, then it might have been stolen. There was a gentleman near me when I was over there- if I could please watch the CCTV back?'

The lad paused.

'I'll just go get my manager.'

Silva waited as he left, wondering what she would say now: "*Yes, this man stole my financial independence and the hopes I had of fulfilling my dreams.*" She grinned despite herself, unsure how that would go down to this manager.

A woman in a spotless white blouse came out from the back. The young lad resumed his post at the bar, albeit his back a little bit straighter and he busied himself with a filthy cloth, wiping down the counter.

'Hello, how can I help you?'

'Hi, I erm, would like to see your CCTV from about six weeks ago, please. I think someone stole something from me, and I need to see who it was.'

'Madam,' the woman began. 'I'm terribly sorry. Data protection laws prevent us sharing that with you without a very valid purpose, and in any case, you would probably need to be a police officer to have a valid reason. I suggest you speak to the police and they can come back.'

'Please, you don't understand. It's important.' Silva said, almost crying. 'I just- it wasn't a theft- so much as – I met someone here. And I would like to see him again.'

The manager sighed, 'this isn't a lonely-hearts club, madam. I can't help you with that, but if he's a regular, come for a dance this evening and see if you recognise him. I'm sorry I cannot do more for you,' she said. 'But please stay for a soft drink on the house with my compliments,' she turned to her employee. 'You can go on break when Tye gets in.'

'Cheers.' The lad said.

'Thank you,' Silva said, not wanting to admit that the

reason she needed the CCTV was that she had been too drunk at the time of conception to go along with the manager's plan, and would be highly unlikely to recognise him now. Would the bloke recognise *her* if he were here? Maybe. He had been pretty drunk too. And what if he did see her and they did it over again? At what point did she tell him he had left her with more than he bargained for?

She accepted a lemonade from the lad behind the bar, thanked him, and drank it slowly, considering her options.

As far as Silva saw it, she was having a bad day; no job- and no one would hire her pregnant, and most, by the time she was ready to go on maternity leave, wouldn't see her as eligible for it. No father to speak of to help her somehow bring up a child that two days ago she hadn't even been aware was inside her body. She declined a call from Eric, her business partner, too ashamed to tell him any of what was going on with her just now.

'Just to let you know, madam... the CCTV around the ladies' hasn't worked in about a year, so even if we could show it to you...it would just be a black screen. Sorry. I probably shouldn't tell you that, but you look so sad.'

Silva smiled at him. 'Thank you. that's very kind of you – thanks for all your help today.' She dropped a few pound coins in the tip jar for his kindness; what he had told her did lift a giant weight off her shoulders at least; there was nothing further she could do and she didn't want to be tied to a stranger – she only wanted to know *who it was.*

*

Silva turned up to Layla's coffee lounge, where she found Layla patiently teaching a new barista how to make foam art. She looked ready to blow a fuse, but when she saw Silva, she smiled.

'Please take a coffee- they're all nice, just art practices. Would only either down them or waste them otherwise. Oh - is caffeine okay with you? Sorry...'

Silva took one gratefully, 'Layla, I don't know yet what I can and can't eat, mate. Caffeine is essential at this precise moment.' Silva said, a bit too truthfully; she knew to avoid soft cheeses and certain seafood and that was about it but her budget stretched to neither of those things at that point anyway.

Layla told her staff member to practice without her and left another in charge of the till, and, taking a coffee for herself, sat down with Silva.

'Look at you go, La-la! So professional.'

'Yeah. They're good, those two. Just lack a bit of confidence, is all. My barista keeps foaming dicks on the lattes, look.'

Silva snorted as she saw what she had picked up. 'At least this dick can't land me in any more trouble.'

'Oh Silv, how did seeing Simi go?'

'She has nothing for me. And I don't feel like I can get a job then suddenly go off needing maternity leave – I'm in a right mess, aren't I?'

'I was so sure Simi would help you,'

'Yeah, I know, but no joy. Then I decided to humiliate myself further and nipped into the nightclub where The Event happened, see if they could share some CCTV... but that's a no-go too. They suggested I called the police.'

Layla bent forward laughing, 'oh goodness, did you tell them why you were there?'

'No, I managed to get away without doing so – the manager would not have seen the funny side. She did suggest I come back to scout the poor git out later- if only she knew she'd suggested I stake out the father of my baby, what on earth would a stranger say to that?!'

Layla was choking on her coffee by this point, and Silva was giggling too. She shook her head.

'Sorry to interrupt, but look what I did, Layla!' the foam art girl said, carefully carrying it over. Her art was now a swan, almost perfect. Layla beamed at her, said well done, and asked her to clear up ready for closing time. She looked at Silva again.

'I think standing over her all afternoon *might* have put her off. My bad. Still new to managing people.'

'You're doing good, Lay. She was so pleased to show you that, they aren't scared of you and they're doing a good job.

Sounds perfect to me.'

'Thanks. Yeah, I'm pleased with my staff, especially Opal, even with the foam dicks,' she said quietly. She had a soft smile as she said Opal's name.

'Do you fancy her a bit?'

'Ssssh! Silv. She's straight. Yes, cute, but married – and I'm taken, remember?'

Silva rolled her eyes fondly in response.

'Right. Your problem. I'm happy to give you any shifts I can in here…I feel like your best plan is to do as much as you can while physically able, and save up. The government aren't going to help you much past statutory - you own your flat, you're out of luck unless you sell it…' Layla said. 'You did just start a business though, and it feels like in your panic you forgot about that and completely lost faith in yourself?'

Silva released a deep breath. Her flat was the last thing she had from her father; well, just about enough money to buy it from his estate, anyway. She wasn't going to give it up, not after she had gutted it of the filthy carpets and disgusting stained walls the previous owners had left her, and filled it with the very little she could afford.

'Then once you've had the baby… I don't know. It's difficult. But you've got this. For now, coffee and cake, if there is any left on the counter, then life. One step at a time. Yes?'

'Yes.' Silva agreed. She tried to smile. Layla was helping her – as much she hated asking for it. Cake sounded like a *really* good idea to her, so she took Layla's cake and her advice, and tried to ignore the panic levels rising in her heart.

CHAPTER 4

Twelve weeks into her pregnancy, Silva went to make a coffee in the morning and found no milk. She was down to one cup of coffee a day and cherished that one caffeinated thing with all she had, the one thing she could count on after the appalling sickness left her, to make her feel all in order again. What she did find, however, was double cream leftover from her birthday cake (which she, uncharacteristically, had eaten most of). She poured cream into her coffee, and a few moments later felt her life change.

This is the best thing ever, she thought, as there was no one to tell; Layla had gone out to work hours ago, and Silva suddenly felt very lonely and very hungry, as she pulled everything sweet out of the cupboards that she could feasibly make a meal out of. She ended up with porridge made with cream, full of raisins, golden syrup and banana. Jake might have even been proud of the concoction, she thought with a little pang. Well, until she found the peanut butter and added that in, then he would have been disgusted.

She sat with her porridge and looked at her first-ever ultrasound scan. A monochrome blur that you had to kind of squint to understand, to decipher that there was someone in there. Her baby's first photo, but not one she had any inclination to put on the internet for all to see; frankly, she wasn't up for the questions, and it was sort of liberating to *not* share something with the whole wide world. She had known a friend who was happily married and not said a word until the baby was out, and Silva wanted to give that a try. It wasn't a secret she would be able to hide for that long; her waist was already beginning to widen, she thought mutinously. At the very least she had to tell her mum. Reflecting on the day before, it couldn't possibly have been any worse;

'Is the father not joining us today?' the sonographer had asked with a raised eyebrow. Silva was in a bad mood at this point, having just dealt with a horrible customer, not to mention bursting for a wee she wasn't allowed to have and forgot to put any filter in place when she replied.

'No, actually, but if you find him, please let me know. I'll be sure to advise him I'm pregnant, that he will need to set up a generous direct debit of child support as well as lavish me with gifts and oh yeah – probably inform him of my name?' The sono-grapher looked a bit shocked. 'Sorry, I didn't mean to snap. Just a bad day. But no, he won't be present at all, you can please note that down in my file or whatever you do.'

The sonographer had pursed her lips and said 'okay, not to worry,' in a tone that Silva felt meant "I am judging you harshly, we both know it, but I'm not doing it obviously enough to war-rant a complaint."

Sometimes, Silva thought, *medical professionals are just play-ground bullies somehow clever enough to pass the exams needed to wear hospital scrubs.*

The real clincher had been being weighed; Silva wasn't sure what she was ready to hear but "almost dangerously underweight" was not it. Silva had been piled up with leaflets and advice and meal plans and felt like crying and going to sleep but she couldn't, she had a client to see in the office...

Silva brought herself back to her porridge and the scan of the baby in her womb that had already turned her life upside down. She tried not to worry about where she was going to find the money for all the things babies needed; hoped she could find them free or cheap from people who had been there, done that, now wanted to get rid of all the stuff that came with it. She also tried not to worry about feeding herself all the things the hos-pital wanted her to eat, let alone how she would feed a baby... and if now was an appropriate time to call her mother. She dialled before she could talk herself out of it.

'Hi, Mum. It's me.'

'Who?'

'Very funny.' Silva said and rolled her eyes. She was an only child.

'I know. How are you, darling?'

'I'm okay, Mum. How are you?'

Her mum answered with some tales of Spain and how beautiful it was, how perfect the men were, how silly she was to stay in England, the usual stuff. Silva savoured the last of her creamy coffee.

'It's good to hear you're happy, Mum. Listen, I have some news...'

'Ooh, who is he?'

'Ha, not quite that. I'm pregnant, Mum.'

'Oh, wow, I wasn't expecting that - congratulations, who's the father?'

'I don't know him. He was a one-night-stand. It doesn't matter to me.'

'Of- oh, erm, right, darlin', this is a lot to take in. If you're happy, I'm happy.' Silva could tell that was a lie as her mother said it. 'How far along are you?'

'12 weeks, just had my first scan. All fine, she just said to eat more.'

'Good, good, yes you should eat more. Your lovely slim figure is about to get ruined by the baby anyway, might as well kiss it goodbye now.' Joyce said, the first honest thing she had said on the call.

'Yeah, sure. Well. Just wanted to tell you, I'm due in May, I know this isn't how you would have wanted things to happen for me but- it just is how it is. And I'm happy.'

'Good, darlin, good. You let me know if you need anything – I don't have anything left from when you were little but I can probably give money if you need it – but yeah. Good luck.'

Good luck? thought Silva. The woman who gave birth to me and raised me is about to be a grandmother and all she has is good luck?!

24

'Thanks, Mum.' Silva said instead of what was actually in her head.

'No worries.' Her mother said, not detecting any of the sarcasm Silva poured into her voice. 'Right, I've got to go, we are off on a road trip for the weekend. It was lovely speaking to you – I will see you soon! Bye!'

Silva threw her phone onto the sofa and watched it bounce off a cushion. She took a deep breath. Her relationship with her mother had always been tenuous, more so since she had been a teenager, even worse a teenager grieving for her father, and since her mother had upped and left, giving her an inheritance to buy somewhere to live, it had been practically non-existent. Silva had called because well – that's what you did. It was big news, but she was hoping for...what? Excitement? Her to suddenly dash home and want to be a doting grandmother?

That was never going to happen, but it would have been nice.

What is it you actually want, Silv? She asked herself as she got up to put her cup and bowl in the dishwasher.

I want to feel like I'm looking after myself, like I'm a half-decent parent; not the kind that would think the phone call we just had was perfectly fine. If my baby calls me to tell me she's pregnant – over a certain age, of course- I want to be happy for her, to help her, to not have her worry like I am about where things are going to come from, and shit – I certainly wouldn't hear that she was underweight and suggest that it's ok, because she can give up on her body now...

Silva was crying as she thought about this, retreating to the sofa under a blanket, realising how if a friend felt like this, was underweight, then... she would feed them, as, she knew with a pang of guilt, Jake and Layla had been trying to do for a fair while now, but she had always stopped them. Always on the go, never time to eat or worry about that because well, at some level, she didn't think she was worth it, and that made her cry even harder. She didn't feel like full cream in coffee should have been a mind-blowing experience. She felt like it should have been a nice treat or a bonus if you happen not to have any milk in the house. When she eventually felt like she could move again, Silva dug

out the info sheets the hospital had given her; they were effect-
ively just balanced meals, things she could make or find out how
to, she just hadn't invested that kind of time in doing it in years.
Maybe not since her dad was alive; she had liked cooking then,
had curves that she'd started to learn to love, but then grief
swallowed her and she couldn't stomach much after that. At this
point in her life, she thought, she was ready to feel nurtured. She
-almost- gagged as she thought it, but it was true, or it felt true,
and that was all she had just then.

And so, for the first time in a long time, Silva wrote a shopping
list, and she went and got it all as cheaply as she could, and she
began to learn to fall in love with food.

*

A few weeks later...

Eric had noticed something was up, of course he had, and since
Silva hadn't volunteered the information, he decided to extract
it.

'You're looking different these days, babes.' He said to
broach the topic, handing her a Pain au Chocolat.

Silva took it gratefully, put it on a plate and tore a bit off. 'How
so?' she asked with her mouth full.

Eric took a deep breath. 'I don't know what's been going on
with you...so don't take this the wrong way. You have a real colour in your cheeks. Your clothes fit a little better – although you
could do with some new ones – and you have just acted differ-
ently, too. More focused in some ways but in others, I lose you to
the unicorns and fairies.'

He had even noticed how amazing her boobs were looking, despite not having the straight-man desire to do anything about it.
He thought better of saying so, unsure of her reactions for the
last few weeks.

'Eric, I'm pregnant.' Silva said.

Eric didn't react at first; Silva could almost see the cogs in his
business brain turning, but he seemed to shake himself, and
hugged her.

'Congratulations- that's great. It certainly seems to suit

you.' he said with a smile.

Silva flushed with pride. 'Thank you. Now, I know... this is going to be confusing for business. We'll still make it work. I'll just have a new responsibility,'

'You make it sound like you're buying a spaniel, love.'

Silva rolled her eyes and grinned. 'Quiet. I think we are going to be okay? I'm sorry I didn't tell you before now.'

'Babes, they are going to have to be. How far along are you?'

'Almost twenty weeks.'

Eric looked at her in shock. 'How did you keep that a secret??'

'You might have the best eye for detail I've ever known, but you miss key stuff, such as me not drinking anything for the last few months, sneaking off mid- decorating to puke in the client's nice clean toilet and my stomach expanding.'

'Oh, yeah.' he said. In truth, with how busy they had been, and how often he seemed to be round his new boyfriend's, he probably wouldn't notice if she had given birth in his living room, so seldom had he seen his own sofa. 'But you've been working so hard, there has to be rules and things...'

'Nah, there doesn't. Mama needs to work, and I rest plenty - I will make sure you know if things get too much. For now- I need the money. As much as I wish I could shove her in a drawer to sleep, apparently health visitors get funny about that these days.'

'Yeah, but... let me look up pregnancy guidelines before you do anything silly like breathe in fumes you shouldn't. I wish you'd told me sooner.'

'Me too.' Silva agreed, feeling like a weight had lifted from her shoulders. *Why did she ever think Eric wouldn't have been kind about this?*

Silva took a deep breath and followed him to their client's ready-to-be-transformed living room.

*

Despite her hopes, fatigue was catching up with Silva by her twentieth week of pregnancy. Her life had become eat-work-sleep, repeat, and online shopping for cheap clothes and food was part of life now. The sound of her letterbox made her leap out of what had felt like a deep sleep.

'It will probably just be sodding bills again, don't know why I'm getting up,' Silva grumbled to herself, actually hoping it would be the sequinned shrug she had bought in a moment of wide-eyed longing.

It was neither bills nor a shiny parcel. Silva bent to pick up a bright yellow envelope and opened it where she stood.

'You are invited to Michelle's baby shower and gender reveal party! Details overleaf. SILVA please bring some ingredients for virgin cocktails for our girly afternoon! Michelle can't wait to see you. Please RSVP.'

Silva suddenly felt like she could sleep another 9 hours and not feel rested. The baby shower was a week away, just into Christmas week. She groaned and went into the kitchen, finding, to her surprise, Layla.

'Good morning, Silv.'

'La-la! You're home?'

'Yeah. My morning off, isn't it. I've started letting the girls have more rope and they're doing great. Trouble is, I don't know what to do with free time now.'

Silva smiled and flipped the kettle switch down. 'You can take the piss out of this if you like.'

Layla took the invite from her. 'Paper party invites? What is this, a child's party? Oh, gender reveal? URRRRRGGHHHHHH. WHY?'

'I know. Promise me you won't put me through anything like this.'

'Can't think of anything worse, babes. Virgin cocktails. Ain't nothing virgin about a baby shower is there.' Layla snorted. 'Are you going?'

Silva sighed as she put a spoonful of coffee into a clean-ish mug.

'I don't know. I really don't want to. I already panic about affording to buy for my own kid, let alone someone else who doesn't actually need to have things bought for her- she is always on bloody holiday, plus I'm going to get there and they'll see my bump and I just can't be bothered to have the conversation over and over, they aren't the kind of friends who would let it go either and I just....meh. You know?'

'Oh I know Silv. I wouldn't even consider it. I don't like you enough' she teased. 'Look, I know you're worried about upsetting people by not turning up but honestly, when was the last time you saw her?'

'A year ago, maybe? But it might be nice to have a mum-friend...'

'I've met her, Silv, she won't be the sort of mum-friend that will help you. Her kid will have a more expensive wardrobe than both of us put together, and all the best toys, and she will make you feel bad about it. Your kind of mum- friends will be more like you. Real people with what they can afford and loving the experience, not just *showing* the experience. Bloody gender reveal. They know what reproductive organ is on the ultrasound picture, not who the baby is or who they're going to be. And they expect you and the other guests to provide the food? That's not a party, that's a cop-out by lazy rich people. Fair enough if they can't afford to cater it but they can, they don't need a community effort. Don't feel bad about this.' Layla's cheeks were flushed and Silva was grinning at her as she poured milk into her mug and helped herself to biscuits.

'Well, I don't anymore. Thank you.'

'Are you panicking about money?'

'Yeah, a bit. I need to somehow buy furniture. Baby bits. My Mum said she would help where she can, so hopefully, she will send some cash... I have a few clothes I couldn't resist and some well-paid client homes coming up, decorating a wedding too... so I should be ok. Just a struggle I wasn't expecting to have to deal with but I'm halfway there, I should really start getting used to it.'

'You're going to be fine, Silv. It's been really lovely watching you...grow? Sorry, that sounded like I'm a creepy Wellness guru. But I mean it. You're eating and you're loving it. You have a glow about you which probably comes from sleeping half the day and eating all of the chocolate but I love it. I think this is good for you, even if it's really hard.'

Silva felt a strange gurning smile reach her face and fought back tears. Layla squeezed her shoulder.

*

At her twenty-week scan, Silva realised would never be ready for how cold the ultrasound goop was and how much it didn't help her full bladder, and she jumped every time.

'You're having a girl. And she looks good. I'm pleased to see you've put on some weight.' The sonographer said. Silva smiled. Her guesses had been correct. She wiped the goop off herself and hobbled to the toilet, where she took a deep breath in the mirror after relieving herself.

'I can't wait for you to come out,' she whispered to her stomach. 'It feels like a lonely life until then.' She sighed.

*

Later, on her sofa and bored, Silva picked up her phone and scrolled social media. It was a habit she had nearly broken but that evening, she was sad. She went through the motions of checking her Mum's page and a couple of friends, put an update on for the business, although Eric was so much better at that than her and then allowed herself to peek at Jake's profile. He was tagged in various photos from various trips out, each with a beautiful blonde girl on his arm. In a few of the photos, they were kissing. The Grand Canyon stretched out behind them like a different planet. Sunburn touched Jake's shoulders but other than that, he looked perfect. Silva felt a twinge in her stomach that she knew had nothing to do with the baby growing inside it. Jake looked so happy and well-adjusted to his new life, which given that he had never lived away from his mum before, even for uni, was surprising to Silva. *Look at you, all grown up,* she thought. She searched the blonde woman, Meg Andrews, according-ing to the tagged photo, for any sign of a ring on her finger or a swell to her belly, any sign that Jake had grown up fast for a reason. She scrolled to a picture of Jake trying to pet a raccoon in a zoo and laughed, automatically adding a 'laugh' reaction to the post before realising what she had done. As she stared at the screen trying to decide if it was suspicious to delete it, a message popped up from Jake.

'Laughing at my fear, I see?' he had written, lightning-fast. Silva looked at the time and did mental maths; he was likely on his lunch break. She smiled in spite of herself.

'Sorry, stranger. Was reminding myself what you looked like and that one cracked me up. You look like you're having fun,' she typed back.

'The best time. Miss you though. Wish you were here to visit.' Jake replied. Silva sighed. The plan had been that she and Layla would take a week off to visit, but then Silva's pregnancy had put paid to that and Layla didn't want to fly on her own.

'Me too. It's too quiet round here and there's no one to magic up dinner from nothing but leave me loads of washing up.' Silva teased, her heart rate rising. *He has a girlfriend, don't get too excited.* She chided herself.

'Ha! I think that's a compliment, maybe?! I've got to run but have a fab Christmas. Say hi to Layla. Xxxxx' Jake typed back and disappeared offline. Silva counted the kisses he had typed and let herself have three seconds to imagine they were real and then shook herself gently. Dreamland was lovely but she had a baby to grow, and she was hungry.

*

'MERRY CHRISTMAS!' Eric yelled as he pulled a cracker with Layla. It was Christmas day and Layla, Eric and Silva were hanging out together. Layla didn't particularly celebrate Christmas and had no family she spoke to anymore, and Eric had a similar story but loved sherry and Christmas pudding, and Silva's mother hadn't bothered showing up. Upon hearing that Eric would be working, Silva had invited him over and together they were ploughing through a boxset of The Walking Dead.

'Silva, we have a surprise for you. Er, let's do this now before we're too drunk.'

'Deal.' He agreed, getting up and then layered up against the cold outside.

Silva narrowed her eyes at them both but didn't say anything. It was the weirdest Christmas she had ever had but she was loving how it felt natural; no one had argued, everyone agreed on the telly. They each enjoyed their favourite bits of Christmas and forgot the rest; for Eric, that was food and drink. For Layla, it was present-giving and for Silva… she didn't honestly mind what she was doing, because she was with two of her favourite people. A few minutes later Eric and Layla returned with enormous wrapped presents.

'We already swapped gifts,' Silva said, confused.

'We know you said you didn't want anything like this… no baby shower… but we wanted to…' Layla paused, choosing her words carefully, 'to give the baby some things from us. We love you.'

Eric placed the packages as gently as he could down, trying not to reveal how heavy they were. His chest puffed with pride at what they had done.

'You shouldn't have, guys.' Silva bit her lip, hating to admit how touched she was. She felt through the paper to see if she could guess what things were and control her reaction.

'NO GUESSING! Open them!' Layla barked.

Silva did. The first contained a Moses basket full of amazing things; a sling, a cellophane parcel full of baby clothes in neutral colours and some in rainbow (the perfect match of Layla's calm nature and Eric's extravagance), and a baby monitor. The second contained a very heavy flat-pack cot with storage and changing space and the third was a car seat.

'Jesus, guys, this is exactly what the wise men should have brought Mary.' Silva said. 'I'm touched. I can't accept this.'

'Well tough, Silv.' Eric said, grinning. 'Believe it or not, most of it is second-hand and we did well. Please take it. You have given us so much, not to mention opening your home to me at Christmas. Let us give you something back.'

Layla was eyeing him, willing him not to say the word 'help'.

When he finished speaking, she nodded at him and accepted a hug from Silva.

'It's all going to be okay, Silv. Told ya.'

Silva smiled and for the first time, started to believe that.

CHAPTER 5

'I think this baby is coming NOW!' Silva yelled to no one at all, partly because she had pictured saying it like she was in a film, and partly because vocalising it made it all suddenly seem so real. Her whole body felt was in a state of emergency. She could feel herself shaking, her blood pulsing in every direction, her palms sweating and her head throbbing. She used the toilet for the fourth time in an hour. She hated feeling so vulnerable, the panic of needing to get to hospital fast and alone making her feel frantic. The ambulance service told her to sit and wait, that they were on hours and hours of delays, could her partner take her down if she needed to come in?

She was sure she would feel bad later for her response to that question, but at that moment in time her thoughts were else-where, with panic and anxiety and wondering if she could pre-tend to not be in labour and get a taxi?

Her phone rang. Layla.

'Hello?'

'How are you feeling, Silv? You didn't look too hot this morning. Well, you did, sweaty and gross, actually.'

Silva closed her eyes and braced herself. 'I think I'm in labour. The ambulance people won't come out for hours yet. I don't know how far along I need to be for hospital to take me but...'

'Calm down. Have you had any contractions yet? Have your waters broken?'

'Erm, the gooey stuff has happened...'

Layla retched a tiny bit and hoped Silva hadn't heard. She had.

'Contractions?'

'Sporadic, I guess. I just don't feel right, though, all hot and sweaty and anxious and weird.'

'Okay. I'm going to come home and time them for you. I'll leave one of the girls in charge. Hey, it's literally Mayday!' Layla laughed. May 1st, of course Silva's baby would choose that date.

'Layla, you don't have to, it'll be okay, I jus-'

'You haven't asked me. I've volunteered. I'll see you in a bit. Want any food? Of course you do.' Layla said and hung up.

Silva closed her eyes and started to weep.

Layla arrived home shortly afterward and dropped a croissant from her coffee shop onto Silva's lap and popped to her bedroom, returning with a notebook, by which point Silva was pale, her teeth clenched in pain.

'On cue. Nice.' She noted the time and started a stopwatch. They passed the time by watching more of The Walking Dead, which did help Silva take her mind off the pain until the pain was all there was and Layla was easing Silva into the passenger side of her car – Layla didn't own one – and was driving them both to hospital, in a mad rush. It felt as though they were in their own localised time zone where every second felt like an eternity.

It took half an hour of begging before the maternity ward would admit them, but being horizontal wasn't a great deal more comfort.

'What the holy hell am I doing, La-la? I'm not ready for this. I'M NOT EQUIPPED FOR THIS. I'm self-employed, skint, I don't know who the father is. I GOT KNOCKED UP IN A NIGHT-CLUB and I just CANNOT DO THIS.' Silva screamed.

Layla held back the urge to shout at her; she had never done this for anyone before.

'Silva...'

'I know. I wanted to be empowering about all of this. Women going it alone and all that stuff but it's so hard and I'm so scared and...'

'Silv...'

'Yeah?'

'Sometimes you need to learn that empowerment comes

from accepting support. You're not alone. It's all going to be okay. Trust me.'

The doctor walked in at that moment, unceremoniously checked Silva's progress, told her it wouldn't be much longer, and walked out again.

'He could at least have bought me a drink first.'

'Like the father did?' Layla quipped with a raised eyebrow. They both roared with laughter.

'Labour isn't meant to be this funny,' a midwife said to them with a confused grin as she strode in. Layla repeated the joke with explanation while Silva's cheeks went redder and redder, and the midwife laughed louder than they had. Silva liked her instantly and relaxed. The midwife did a few more checks on her, reassured her, then left.

'How does your body feel, Silva?' curiosity had won out over Layla's squeamish side.

'Like I need the toilet. Like I've been taken over by aliens. Like I want to get this baby out of me so at least we can face each other and work out where we go from here.'

'I'm not sure the baby will-'

'Yeah I know, but it's easier to reason with someone tangible than wander round chatting nonsense to your stomach, isn't it?'

'Fair enough.'

Half an hour later, Silva was in the worst pain of her life and felt like her soul was trying to leave her body. She guessed that that was what they meant by 'you'll know when you're ready to push' – she just hadn't expected it to feel like a battle royale over *which* of them left her body. A few minutes - or hours, who knew - of hardcore pushing later, she was holding a bloody, wriggling, screaming mess. At any other point, Layla would have made a joke about how disgusting newborn babies looked, but when Silva looked at her, her eyes were full of pride and love. Silva burst into tears at the sight of her best friend feeling the same way that she did.

'Silva, she's not that ugly. I'm sure she will look like you soon enough.' Layla said teasingly.

Silva snorted. 'Shut up. It's just overwhelming.'

'Yep. That's the word, all right.'

Silva lay for hours with her baby, long after Layla had to get back to work to cash up even though it was long after closing, and long after Silva had been patched up and then told to stay overnight to make sure they were both ok and could get the knack of feeding, which second to childbirth felt like the most difficult thing Silva had ever attempted. But she was in awe of her baby's tiny nose and her little, thin old-lady fingers, wrinkled by nothing but a long time in the bath of her belly. She didn't want to put the baby down to go for a wee, which would be when a father could be there to watch over their child, and it struck Silva as her blood still screamed with hormones that this was it – her and her baby against the world now.

Eventually, a nurse took the baby and barked at her to get up to use the toilet and get moving so her blood didn't clot. Silva hated every second of not being next to her baby. When she returned after the most painful visit to the toilet of her life to a peaceful, sleeping infant; much to her annoyance, she hadn't been missed, the nurse put her in her cot.

'Enjoy a hot drink while you can, love. This will probably be your last. And eat,' she said kindly, but firmly. Silva's eyes filled.

'What are you going to call her?' the nurse asked, more gently.

'Rose.' Silva said. The name had been circulating in her brain, and as she said it, it fit the baby, her cheeks flushed rose red, her lips pouted open like the bud of a rose, and of course, her petal-soft skin that Silva still couldn't believe had been made by her own body.

'Beautiful.' The nurse said, smiling. 'What do you want for dinner?'

'Toast.' Silva said. She had heard new mothers in the ward say it tasted amazing after their labours, and when it arrived a bit later she was pleased to find that that was indeed like nothing else she had ever eaten.

*

Six months later...

The nurse had been correct, Silva had given up making herself a hot drink as even if Rose was asleep and she had the chance to drink it, she either fell asleep too or forgot about it. Layla had brought home enough slow-release carbs to keep her going, despite them both joining Rose in becoming nocturnal when she was just a few weeks old.

Silva got out of the shower and into clean pyjamas to find Layla cuddling a sleeping Rose, a look of peace on her face. She smiled, seeing that Layla was also fast asleep.

She was surprised to see Jake also sitting on her sofa, and she made as excited a sound as she could without waking the sleepers. Silva's heart was in her throat; a year of his absence hadn't taken the edge off her feelings for him.

He was perched awkwardly on the sofa, drinking tea and waiting for Layla to let him have a go at holding Rose but Silva could see that that was unlikely. Her heart hurt, picturing Jake as a father. He would be good. She cocked her head toward the kitchen and he followed her.

'It's lovely to see you.' Silva said as they hugged.

'You, too, Silv, sorry I've not been around through all of this.' He said, resisting the urge to open her fridge to distract himself from how... awkward he felt. How beautiful Silva looked; cheeks flushed from the shower, hair at its calmest before it dried and went wild, and pregnancy and childbirth seemed to have made her look a bit...fuller. Healthier. *Happier,* he thought.

'Not at all, Jake. It means a lot that you're here now. Now look in the fridge, I know you're dying to. There is actual nice food in here, I'm a changed woman.'

Jake grinned and opened the door, suitably impressed.

'Very good. Do you want me to make something? Something easy to reheat when you're starving and tired?'

Silva blinked back tears. 'Please! Then I promise I will

gently get Rose off Layla so you can have a cuddle.'

'You don't need to do that. I don't know what I'm doing.'

'I do. Rose needs to meet her uncle Jake properly, you'll be fine.'

Calling him 'uncle' Jake stung both of them in the same place, but neither of them acknowledged or admitted it.

Rose broke the tension by waking up with a cry.

'She's hungry... I'll just...' Silva said, a little sad for the distraction but also pleased Jake would be too busy in the kitchen to witness her feeding, not that she felt awkward about it but... okay, she felt awkward about it in front of him. Not because she liked him, but because he was male, she told herself.

Layla took her opportunity to shower and change her clothes into something not baby-sick covered. Rose settled quickly and Jake, a few minutes later, popped his head round the door from the kitchen, completely forgetting that Rose was feeding.

'Oh, sorry, I just wanted to know if you wanted a cup of tea?'

Silva flushed at the same time Jake did.

'Yes please.' Silva was already used to flashing everyone and anyone but...she felt weird about it being Jake, who felt weird about feeling weird about it.

Jake came in with her tea as Silva was burping Rose. They avoided each other's eyes for a minute despite being sat next to each other on what suddenly felt like a very small sofa, but when Silva was sure Rose was winded, she passed a muslin to Jake and then, let him take her.

Silva smiled as he took Rose carefully; suppressing a giggle as he suddenly grew extra elbows. Her heart thumped a bit harder than usual. She ignored it, blaming hormones, as he settled with the baby and started chatting to her softly. Somehow, it just looked *right* on him, which wasn't a thought that she ever thought she'd have.

'You got a girlfriend right now, Jake?'

'Kind of,' he replied, a curve on his lips. 'Why?'

Silva looked at Rose and raised her eyebrows.

'No, nowhere near that yet,' he said, hurriedly, but he had a softness to his expression as he tickled Rose to make her laugh. Silva shrugged and blinked away the wave of useless hormonal tears she felt coming on.

'Well, one day, you'll make a good dad,' she said.

'Thank you.' he said, smiling at Rose who took the opportunity to vomit back Silva's breast milk onto Jake's stomach.

'And thank you, little lady. I'm going to take that as you like me?'

'That's why I gave you the muslin, idiot.' Silva laughed. Her cheeks were pink again from embarrassment.

Jake laughed too, his head leaning towards Silva's, Rose settling herself on Jake's lap now he had stopped bouncing her and just let her lay and watch him, her eyes drooping.

It felt so much like the old days when they both felt the spark and his heart was beating so fast that when their lips met – and no one could say who made that move – it felt right and both their bodies felt like they had been set alight.

'What smells so good?' Layla asked, breezing in, realising she had interrupted something as Silva and Jake sprang apart, and Rose stirred. Avoiding eye contact, they both remembered with dread that Jake had a girlfriend.

'Dinner,' Jake said. 'Dinner for now and a few bits to stick in the fridge to keep you guys going without me,' his eyes twinkled, 'and yes, Silv, I left you the washing up,' he said, grinning. Silva smiled back sadly.

'Feel free to move in if you'll cook,' Layla said with an awkward smile. She stood, shuffling their weight from foot to foot, nodded at them both, and went back to their bedroom.

Neither Silva nor Jake spoke for a moment.

'I can't - I'm with someone – I'm sorry.' Jake said in a jumble.

'I know – I'm sorry too,' Silva said, although she wasn't sorry it happened, 'and I can't really get into anything anyway… Rose…'

They were both disappointed they had had to stop.

'Yeah. Always the wrong time for us, isn't it.' Jake said with a heavy sadness in his voice.

Silva closed her eyes and took a deep breath, feeling like she had stopped breathing. She had nothing to say to that.

Jake went home after dinner, muttering about emails he had to send, but they all knew: he was off to call his girlfriend.

*

'Mum! Hi!' Silva said with a surprised smile the next day, which at least snapped Silva out of thinking about Jake nonstop.

'Hello darling, don't look so shocked! I have a granddaughter to meet. And a daughter to hug.'

'Let me take your stuff first. Are you moving in?!' Silva said, but her brain couldn't resist thinking, *Rose is six months old and you haven't shown the slightest interest until now...*

'This is me packing light!'

'Of course.' Silva had not inherited her mother's need for choices of clothes.

Her mother set down a suitcase in the hallway, and what looked like a guitar case too.

Silva hugged her mother when she wasn't laden with stuff.

'Rose is asleep, we can talk first. Jake made an awesome casserole if you want some?'

'Oooh, Jake's been here has he? Interesting. I've eaten, but tell me more...'

Silva flushed, the muscle memory of their shouldn't-have kiss still fresh in her memory.

'Yeah. He's home at the moment. Came over to meet Rose and like a sweetheart, made us dinner and some easy-reheat stuff.'

'What a star. I always thought you should be together, you know.'

'I know. He has a girlfriend. No doubt some sophisticated New Yorker who looks magazine-ready. And I have a baby. It's not the right time for any relationship, let alone one with him, Mum.'

'Hmm,' her mother nodded slowly. 'How are you feeling

anyway?'

'Exhausted and terrified. I hear that's pretty standard though,' Silva said and grinned. 'Layla has been fantastic, though,'

'Yes, she is very patient to live with a new baby, isn't she? You're lucky.'

'I am.' Silva agreed. 'What's in the guitar bag, Mum?'

'Ahh, yes. That's your dad's guitar. I know you said you didn't want it when he passed, but I kept it. I took it with me when I moved. I thought you might change your mind – he used to play to you to get you to sleep when you were a baby – I just thought it might be nice to pass that on to Rose. To remember him.'

Silva openly wept at the thought, and at the sadness that her father would never meet his granddaughter.

'I'm sorry – was it wrong of me?'

'No, it was perfect. I think Rose will love it – she already loves a bit of a boogie to Bowie.' Silva smiled happily. It had been her utter pleasure to realise a few days ago that Rose was too little to care what she was hearing – she had a while before repetitive kid's songs took over their lives – so she had danced around the kitchen in her filthy clothes, covered in sick and sneeze and snot (which was *mostly* Rose's) and just felt free.

'Good.'

An empty moment of silence passed between them with neither sure what to say next.

Silva thought about how her father had taught her to play chords; how to place her fingers in the right places on the frets, how to re-string: "you have to be firm but gentle. The guitar should know you're in charge.", and a tiny bit of piano, but she had never cared for it. "The piano is a different thing. Majestic. It bites you. Needs professionals to tune her as she has expensive taste – much like your mother..." he had said and smirked.

It hadn't occurred to Silva until now that he spoke about the instruments as though they were alive, and she smiled. She sort of agreed, that the hum of a tune from an instrument could be mistaken for a breath or a purr, that when she used to perform a bit and sing on stages the guitar had felt like a member of the band, a friend up there with her.

She remembered her father making up funny words and phrases to get her to remember chords, but none of them came to her now. Maybe they would if she taught Rose to play one day.

It had been a hard year, that year he died. Losing him too soon, unnaturally, and a pregnancy too early on to know how to feel about it – and she was certainly too young to have been pregnant and fatherless at once – but it had been the year she had learnt a lot, she supposed, and ten years later the loss still hurt.

Her father could have been famous – he was a talented musician and singer, and he had toured half the world. She felt like he had let his dreams go and blamed herself – her existence – but what she didn't know is that he simply preferred to spend time with his family; his daughter.

She had learned to guard her heart that year, and that trusting boys was a fool's game because they didn't deal with the consequences of their desires. She had also felt lucky that no one found out; that her father's death had made her mother move almost straight away and meant she could become someone new in a new college, and no one knew about the pain of it all to remind her of why she was sad. She thought of the guitar her mother had brought her and for the first time in years, thinking of her father brought her warmth instead of just pain. She grinned.

If she had made him a grandfather at forty-two, he would have killed her. But now he would have been fifty-two, still young enough to enjoy chasing a toddler around but old enough to be a little more ready for it.

Rose broke Silva's thoughts by crying. Both women stood up and Silva led her mother to Rose's room and scooped up her baby from the cot.

'Nappy change.' Silva said wearily.

'It's pretty in here,' her mother said as Silva got to work on the clean-up. 'Not very pink though, is it?'

'There is more to being a girl than everything being pink, Mum. And more to being a boy than blue.' Silva replied as Joyce took in the details, the white accented accessories that Eric had found (and managed to deliver to her despite being very busy) going cheap on his charity shop and boot sale trawls against the rainbows that Silva had painted on the walls – and the glittery unicorns she hadn't been able to stop herself from drawing and painting too. She was proud of this room, and knew from her design training that babies loved bright colours – Rose regularly stared at the unicorns with amused wonder on her face and would laugh if Silva made it talk.

'Oh, you aren't pushing all that on her, are you? I guess all her clothes are neutral colours too,'

'Well, some are pink. A lot are either Disney outfits that Layla hoarded or just cheap by-the-bag things we found online and washed – she doesn't wear things for long. I'm wondering why all baby clothes aren't just terracotta-brown or off-white because that's what colour it all ends up!' Silva laughed.

'Oh, the joys of motherhood.' Her Mum said.

'And I'm not pushing her into anything,' Silva said, as she pulled a fresh outfit on Rose – the only pink thing she had to make her mum smile – and handed her to her grandmother for the first time. 'I just don't want her thinking pink is her only option to express who she is. She can play with whatever, she can have dolls if she wants them but if she wants to be a messy kid with train sets that's fine too. I'm just not going to bring up a baby housewife on purpose. It's the 21st century, we're past making girls think they have to do what's expected. And that's what pink represents to me. A neat little box of expectations. Same with blue.'

'Hello little Rose, I'm your Nanna Joyce, and you are beautiful,' Joyce said, instantly smitten and choosing to ignore Silva's reasoning. 'She is a beautiful baby, darling.'

'I know. Isn't she just?' Silva said, beaming, trying not to let the sting of her mother's disregard irritate her.

'I'm sorry about what I said. About what your dad would

44

have thought. He would be so proud – and not at all surprised that you're doing this independently.'

Silva let out a breath and unclenched her jaw, releasing tension she hadn't known was big enough to ache.

'Thank you.'

Rose seemed to like her Nanna, and Silva was happy to let them bond so she could answer some enquiring emails and book some appointments for prospective clients. She felt more like herself after doing so; what they never tell you about motherhood, she thought, was that it makes you feel unproductive despite growing and birthing, and nurturing a human life. Or maybe that was just her brain.

'Back to work already?'

'Part-time for the first few months, yeah. I run a business, Mum, I don't have a choice. I don't know how it'll work out – my whole life is blind faith and hope at this stage.'

'What will you do with Rose out on jobs? You can't have her round the paint and chemical fumes, surely?'

'I know. Eric has done a lot on his own – I've done some consults here and drawn up designs but really, I just don't know – unless we hire someone to work with Eric – but I don't know if we can afford that yet. We have a really big job next week – great for the portfolio, a Z-list celebrity's flat with a great big budget and they've let us go wild.'

'Oh, which celebrity? Not that I'd know them…'

'I cannot say Mum. It's under wraps until they put it on their social media pages as a big reveal – it could mean really big things for us.'

'Brilliant.'

Silva nodded, her body tense, hating every word that came out of her mouth next.

'Would you mind staying a bit longer and looking after Rose while we have this big job? So we can get it done and dusted – it will be quick, we have everything ready to go and in the studio, and I'll be home in the evenings if you want to go out…' Silva trailed off as her mum shook her head.

'I have to get back for the weekend – Stefan and I are buying a villa and doing it up to rent out this summer – in fact, I'd love your advice about the décor, or you are welcome to come out and do it and we'll hire you?'

'I think Eric would bite your hand off for that one, Mum. Rose is a bit young for the plane just yet.' Silva said, her heart visiting her knees at breakneck speed.

'Suit yourself, my love,' Joyce said as she squeezed her hand. 'You will figure something out.'

They passed the next couple of days without argument – the longest they had spent together argument free in years – but as soon as her mother left, the weight of her problem settled, and her fears were confirmed: she had to find a way to carry on working and look after her child.

She was terrified.

CHAPTER 6

Silva furiously overpacked Rose's bag. She knew there was no way Rose would need thirty nappies for 6 hours with a childminder, would never go through ten outfits, or three packets of baby wipes, but she didn't quite feel right when she took anything out of the now very heavy bag. She hauled the bag and Rose down the stairs of her flat building, swearing under her breath and sweating, praying if she dropped anything it was the bag.

It was just six hours with a stranger, what could possibly go wrong?

Oh, wait, *everything* could go wrong.

This woman could be a murderer, cannibal, kidnapper, she could run off with Rose... sure, Silva had seen the Ofsted registration and references, read her reviews that all looked genuine enough, and suggested she was not going to do any of those things, simply snuggle her baby for a few hours while also juggling a couple of toddlers of her own. Rachel had been nothing but kind and polite when she had met them the afternoon before. Silva was confident Rose would be fine, but she couldn't stop the fear and her heart pounded a furious drumbeat until she saw Rachel again, who beamed at Rose, who suddenly seemed so small and fragile.

'Oh hello Silva. She's even cuter in daylight! Look at her perfect chubby little cheeks. Come in, we'll get her settled with me first so she doesn't howl when she realises you're leaving. No need to look worried, she will be absolutely fine.'

Rachel took the enormous bag from Silva, and if she noticed that it weighed about as much as a pregnant walrus, she didn't show it.

'I've packed loads, she won't need it all, but I...just in case.'

'I get it. Does the milk need to be in the fridge?'

'It should be okay in the cool bags. Thank you.'

'Perfect.' Rachel said. They sat down on cosy beige sofas. Silva accepted a cup of tea and Rose happily sat in the bouncer she was placed in with no second thought for Silva, as Rachel had Disney Plus on the TV. Silva finished her tea and felt her nerves settle – Rose was fine, as were the toddlers who were sat on the floor with her, investigating their new playmate.

'I'm going to get to work. Thank you for this – I think Rose will be okay, shall I say goodbye?'

'Don't linger over it – she'll get worried.' Rachel said. 'Don't worry about her, truly. If you want an update, just give me a call – I know it's nerve-wracking.'

Silva smiled gratefully, a little of the tension relieved from her shoulders, but leaving her child for the first time tore her heart in two, and she wondered if she should have just taken it out and left it in the bag for Rachel to take care of too. Silva bought takeaway coffee on her way to the office she shared with Eric, a rare treat at the moment. As her heart rate rose with the extra caffeine, she found herself buzzing with *more* fear.

'Hello darling, so nice to see you in clothes again!'

'Oi, cheeky!' Silva said and hugged him, handing him his skinny caramel latte. Eric grinned, brown eyes twinkling and his hair shining with gel – higher than she had seen it for a long time. He had made a real effort – and so had she; the nicest outfit she could fit into post-baby, the first lick of make-up on in months.

'Let's get cracking, shall we?' Eric said, and they did, discussing the strategy they were going to use in their meeting. They both shook with nerves, although Silva's were mostly over Rose and how she was doing.

She took a deep breath and excused herself to call Rachel, receiving her answerphone.

'What's your face about?' Eric asked as Silva returned.

'Childminder isn't answering. What if -?'

'She will be fine, Silv. The childminder is probably tackling one of Rose's famous nappies. Try again in a bit. Meanwhile – I think we're pretty much there, don't you?'

Silva eyed their pitch; beautiful mock-ups of how the flat would look, explanations of why and a write-up of what Coral Evangeline, their celebrity, had discussed with them. They would need to ask if it was okay to use in the pitch, but if Coral said yes, this could mean a lot for them.

'Yes, it looks great. I just hope Coral lets us send it all – nothing in here makes her look bad, if anything, it makes her sound cooler than she actually came across. I think she was hungover.'

Eric grinned at her and checked his watch. They had an hour before a big meeting was due to take place.

'I feel almost human again,' Silva said with wonder. 'There is no one after my tits for their lunch and my brain isn't overloaded.'

Eric rolled his eyes and said, 'and I am definitely not after your tits for my lunch. You're safe.'

Silva laughed and shook her head. 'You're missing out. My milk bar has a five-star rating on Bib Advisor.'

They answered some emails in companionable silence and sent off their magazine pitch to Coral to approve. Her publicist replied so fast they wondered if it was an auto-reply, saying she loved it, send it, and they both did an excited little dance that shook the walls of their little office.

Silva felt a surge of guilt for enjoying something other than being with her child. And another one for thinking that she should feel guilty for doing what she loved – after all, wouldn't she want Rose to have this feeling at work?

Motherhood is complicated, she thought to herself, and then; *understatement of the century.*

'Hello hello,' Layla sang, waltzing into the office. Silva and Eric greeted her happily, Silva feeling a stab of guilt that she hadn't bought their coffee from Layla's shop, rather a large chain next door. She was pleased to have binned the evidence already.

'To what do we owe the pleasure?' Silva asked warmly, hitting send on her last email and enjoying her empty inbox.

'I thought I'd come in to see if you needed me to take Rose while you had your big meeting. I can have her in the shop while I work, honestly, the girls are doing great and we aren't too busy.' Layla said with a proud smile. 'Where is she anyway?'

'I'm trying her out with a childminder,' Silva said, 'I was going to ask you but...you do so much for us already and I felt bad asking.'

Layla looked dejected, and Silva knew her friend well enough to know the glint in her eye meant tears were being held back.

'Oh. Ok. I – don't you trust me?'

'I absolutely do! In fact, I *wish* she was with you. I've been nothing but tense and terrified all day about how she is.'

'Oh Silva, we could have arranged something! We talked about this, how my job and training the girls so well meant I could help you – and vice versa, you would cater big meetings from the café. This hurts, dude. You know how much I love Rose. Why are you throwing cash away on a childminder?!'

Silva felt tears coming as she realised how much harder she had made things for herself without needing to.

'Just ask for fucking help, Silva. I know you find it hard because of your shitty mother. Trust me, I find it hard too – you're not the only one whose family don't understand you, y'know.'

Silva wiped rapidly streaming tears. Eric nervously checked his watch; as empathetic as he was, he didn't think an argument in the office was a good first impression, but he knew much better than to interrupt women arguing. He slipped to their kitchen and filled the kettle, digging out the good cups and biscuits. Twenty minutes to go.

'I am so sorry. I'm an idiot, Layla.'

'Silva, you inspire me so much, your dedication to your dreams is amazing, you're the reason I quit work to start the café. You just don't ask for help when you need to and my goodness you need to. What if I needed help? You wouldn't hesitate to help me if you could...'

'You're one hundred per cent right.' Silva replied. 'I'm so, so sorry. And thank you for all you've done for me – I do appreciate it, you know.'

Layla clicked her tongue. 'Mmmhmm. We'll chat later, Silv. You've got a meeting, and I guess I have a free afternoon to my-self – no Rose to cuddle.' She snapped, turned on her heel and left.

Silva sank into her chair and put her head in her hands and swore.

Eric came in, replaced the painting that had fallen off its hook when Layla slammed the door and patted Silva's shoulder.

'I know this is going to sound strange, but there are much worse problems to have than a best friend who is sad you thought about her feelings and paid someone to look after your baby.'

'I know – but Layla genuinely loves doing it. And I didn't think about that – and now I feel atrocious.'

'Oh, sweetie. She's right, though, you do need to get better at asking for help. I've got some great books on it – don't look at me like that, they're audiobooks you can listen to, do you think I read actual books? – you could have brought Rose today; I wouldn't have minded, and our clients would have to just get over it if it bothered them – it is the twenty-first century and I don't want to do business with anyone who thinks it matters. I'm gay and you're a single mum, together we make a sitcom – you can put milk in bottles, it's not like you're whacking a boob out mid-chat about colour schemes, is it – which would be fine but I feel like you would want privacy for that at least at work – please stop me talking now.'

Silva laughed at Eric and stood to hug him.

'You're right, thank you. I just feel so fucking torn. Having her here would rock – but what about the on-location stuff?'

'We can figure that out – maybe get a couple of pairs of hands in – if project Coral goes well we would do that anyway, wouldn't we – just be pre-empting it is all.'

'And that, Eric, is why I didn't do well in traditional employment. I didn't have a You talking sense at me.'

Eric doffed a pretend hat. 'You would be lost without me. Now please, go sort your face out, you look like we just broke up.' Silva obliged, calling Rachel as she did.

'Everything is fine. Sorry I missed you earlier – my youngest fell over and had a lovely screaming fit which woke Rose and my eldest. Rose is so very sweet. Do you need longer?'

'Actually, yes please. Would another couple of hours be okay please?' Silva said, thinking about Layla – taking her for a child-free drink to talk things through properly.

'Of course, will be my flat rate, see you soon.'

'Is there enough milk?'

'Plenty, sweetheart, she's only had one bottle so far.'

'Amazing, thank you.' Silva said and hung up, emerging from the toilet fresh and clean and with two minutes to spare to read through their notes.

*

'How was the meeting?' Layla asked Silva as she sipped a Daquiri in the bar closest to home.

'It went well I think, they really liked our ideas for them. They'll let us know if they want to hire us – which could go either way but screw it, we showed them a good time.' Silva shrugged. Although her drink was a virgin Pina Colada, it tasted so close to the real thing that her shoulders relaxed and she felt like Layla had at least in part forgiven her for their argument earlier.

'They'll hire you, Silv. I'm sure you did great.' Layla replied. A moment of quiet passed. Silva checked her phone but there were no messages from Rachel.

'Listen, I'm sorry about earlier. It just hurt. I felt like you didn't trust me with Rose.'

'That's not it at all – I just – I don't want to be a burden. You have work to do too, and a life to live – you didn't choose this, I can't expect you to drop everything – you aren't her parent.'

'That's true. But I am here to help and the worst thing I can say is, "sorry but I can't."'

'You're right...' Silva sighed. 'I just feel so serious at the moment. I have someone to take care of and still have to deal with myself too, even when I really don't want to, and I just – I feel like I'm failing. Like I can't do any of this. Like they should do a maturity test when you have a positive pregnancy test, and I would have failed and had to find somewhere for Rose to go.'

'Oh, Silv. Listen to me. You are doing fine. Both you and Rose are clean and fed and for the most part, rested. That's winning in my eyes. You are getting up and doing it despite finding it tough. That makes you a superhero.'

'A superhero with leaky tits and a filthy flat.'

'The flat, my love, has never been properly clean and you know it.'

'Fair point.' Silva said. 'I'm sorry that I hurt you. You're my first port of call in future.'

'Good.' Layla said, smiled and finished her drink. 'Serious talk – and selfish too – Rose may be the only baby I ever get to spend so much time with. It's my pleasure.'

'You'll have a baby one day! You don't know what's around the corner...'

'At the moment, I think I know. I'm losing hope on the dating thing.'

'Did it not work out with Emily?'

'Well, last night while I was at hers and we were having dinner, her ex turned up with a fucking bunch of roses and asked her to marry her...'

'Oh no she did not! What did Emily do?'

'Emily said yes.'

Silva stared at her open-mouthed.

'Yeah. I know. I took my shit and let myself out. That puts the nail in the dating coffin for a while, I think.'

'I'm not surprised. I'm so sorry.'

'Yeah. Probably also why I kicked off so hard today.'

Silva squeezed her hand. 'You'll find someone who would never do that to you. Come on, let's go home and get a takeaway.

Forget all about her.'

'That sounds good to me.'

They gathered their things up and walked to the car. A few minutes into the journey to pick up Rose, Layla stopped dead while scrolling on her phone.

'Silv? It's Coral Evangeline that you were doing the flat renovation for wasn't it?'

'Yeah. It's going to be beautiful. I'm exci-'

'She was just arrested for driving under the influence of drugs.'

Silva's blood turned to ice.

CHAPTER 7

'She put a guy in hospital, Eric. *Of course* they dropped the story.' Eric shook his head as Silva bounced Rose on her knee.

'I'm hoping she keeps us on to do the job though…'

'Yeah. Me too.' Silva replied. 'But it won't be the best thing on our CV of past jobs, will it? The pop star turned criminal?'

'Plenty of celebrities have done very stupid things and come back from it.' Eric insisted. 'Her new home could be ideal for a comeback as a homely girl who has stopped her party life-style.'

'She can't do that from prison though, can she?' Silva countered.

Eric nodded and dropped his head into his hands.

'We bought all of the materials. We haven't been paid.'

'Can we get a refund?'

'On some of it. I just – ARRRRGH. THIS WAS MEANT TO BE OUR BIG BREAK.'

'I know.' Silva said. Rose squirmed, restless. 'I'm going to go get some lunch – what do you want?'

'I'll have a brown paper bag concealing whisky.'

'Don't be such a drama queen. Do you want a sandwich from that hipster café you like?'

'Ooh yeah. The one that thinks it's in New York and hasn't realised it's actually in Essex?'

'Yep. Text me what you fancy, you know I'll forget.'

'Deal.'

Silva wrangled Rose into her pram and left the office, feeling a bit better for the sea breeze – although it was bitterly cold – and leant down to wrap Rose in a little tighter to her blankets. Rose smiled at her mother, which melted Silva's heart instantly.

'Oh kiddo, what are we going to do?' Rose asked her softly. Rose kept smiling, blinking slowly – she would be asleep shortly, Silva knew as she pushed the pram a long route to the café that Eric liked. She wanted the fresh air, a space to think outside of Eric's catastrophizing.

Silva reached the café doors as a voice shouted.

'Oh my goodness, Silva!'

Silva knew that voice. She stopped herself from groaning.

'Hello Michelle! How lovely to bump into you!' Silva lied.

'Bump is the operative word! I'm pregnant again!'

'Ah, congratulations... So sorry I couldn't make it to the last baby shower.'

'No worries darling, I see you were busy yourself... you should have said, we could have gone to classes together, we still could! Our babies have what, 3 months between them? Oh, your baby is gorgeous, what's her name?' Michelle shrilled, and Rose didn't wake up – somehow.

'She's Rose, how about yours?'

'Lily! Haha, how funny, our flower girls! Are you going in for lunch? Want to join us?'

'Errm,' Silva said, unsure what reaction she would get if she told the truth about picking up lunch for work. 'Sure, I can't stay long though...' she said, which was the truth.

'Who's her dad then?' Michelle asked as they waited for a table. Silva was grateful when her answer of "we aren't together" was saved from further questioning by a waitress showing them to a table.

They sat down and ordered, and Silva found herself nodding politely through Michelle's baby talk, hoping that she didn't do this to Layla and Eric. She tried not to, she appreciated that the outcome of a nappy was not fascinating to *her* let alone her friends. Eventually, Michelle said something of interest to Silva.

'We are thinking of getting a proper interior design company in, we just don't have the time to decorate how we would like to, it's such a big beautiful house and it deserves proper time and attention...'

'I may be able to help you there!' Silva cut in, making Michelle blink in shock. She clearly wasn't used to being interrupted. 'I own – co-own an interior design company. You would be welcome to come in and discuss your budgets and needs – we'll work around your schedule and show you our ideas before we put a lick of paint on anything.' Silva said, digging in her pockets for a business card and thankfully, finding one not covered in baby dribble, milk, or her own snack debris.

'Oh wow, thank you. I'll have a look! You might have just saved my life, but you haven't gone back to work *already,* have you?!'

'I co-own. I can't disappear and... I need money! I'm not doing physical stuff yet – meetings, consults, Rose comes too, I think the clients like her.' Silva said, defensive. 'The website has loads of examples of our previous work and testimonials – I'll knock a bit off the price for you if you go with us.'

'Okay, okay, no need to keep going on about it,' said Michelle. *Hypocrite.* Silva thought. *I've just sat through twenty minutes about how Lily is finding being weaned and how perfect your life is. I think you can let me have a minute.*

Outwardly, Silva grinned. 'Thank you for this. I have to make a move – I really hope to see you soon, it was great to see you. This should cover mine.' she said, pulling out a crumpled ten-pound note.

'Ah, that's a shame. Yes, I'll see you soon.' Michelle said, smiling back at Silva in a way that unnerved her. Silva nodded and wheeled Rose's pram to the take-out queue and she bought Eric's sandwich.

At least we have a potential new client, she thought to herself. *The things I do for love and money.*

When she returned to the office to feed Eric, he looked ashen. She put Rose on her playmat for a few minutes while he ate.

'What's happened, then?'

'Coral's PR phoned- they're cancelling everything. We

turned down projects for this. Now our calendar is next to nothing. We're ruined.' Eric said, tears in his eyes.

Silva bent to hug him. 'If it makes you feel any better, I just endured a quick lunch with the world's most boring woman who just bought the world's biggest house apparently- but has a baby and another coming and no time to fix it all up – and I gave her our card… so that could be something?'

'Ah, brilliant.' Eric said, his face softening. 'We've just got to get back out there and get our hustle on.'

'Exactly that.' Silva said. She bent down to sort out Rose's nappy before she screeched about it. 'We are going to be ok.' She said, mostly to herself. She had to believe it would all work out, that this strange by-the-seat-of-her-pants life was going to work out for them all.

But as she replied to emails on her phone – Rose had the laptop with Peppa Pig on it - Silva made a mental note to buy a cheap telly she could play DVDs on for her for the office – she felt a rush of terror wash over her.

She wasn't sure at all if anything would be okay at all.

CHAPTER 8

'So Michelle psyched you out, then?' Layla asked as Silva sat down, having settled Rose to sleep for the third time in an hour.

'I don't know if we can blame it on her. Or if it was just a terrible day.'

'It probably didn't help though, did it? Still, at least she might be a half-decent contract to make up for the Coral fiasco.'

'Fingers crossed. She's coming in tomorrow to talk about what she wants. I'm not sure what to do with Rose, though, I feel like Michelle will judge me hard if she's at work with me because *perfect Michelle* doesn't need to go back to work, she can just surf around town all day on her husband's cash, while she makes perfect babies for him and terrorizes the mums who are all slowly losing our minds and don't own knickers without holes or jumpers without sick – or shit – stains on them.'

'Are you finished?' Layla said, trying not to laugh. 'I can take Rose,' she said before Silva had a chance to feel completely useless.

'Thank you. I can keep her for the morning, and drop her to you in the afternoon? I feel so completely pathetic, Lay. I shouldn't be ashamed of my little girl. I'm so sorry.'
Layla looked at her friend and took a deep breath.

'You *aren't* ashamed of her. You are just busy. And you want to do the right thing to win your client, and this is it. I know you will make it up to me, and that you will do whatever I need you to do – you know, how you always do the food shop at the minute, and the housework, because I'm too tired to move when I get in – we are looking after each other, here,' she said.

'I know, I just... I watch other parents just hand over their baby to the dad or their own parents and think "that would be *so* nice" but in saying that I've forgotten that I did choose this life for myself. That I like my independence. I just find asking for help so damn hard. And it doesn't help that my mum doesn't help -at all – and I don't feel even emotionally supported by her. She's meant to want to be a grandparent, right, but she couldn't zip back to Spain fast enough and I hate how much I need you, Lay. It isn't fair on you at all. You didn't sign up to co-parent.'

Layla just looked at Silva again for a moment- partially for effect, partially because she was working up the energy to have this conversation, and was exhausted from her day of hauling in deliveries for the shop and serving for eight solid hours, and she was irritable with hunger on top of all of it.

What Silva saw in her friend's eyes in that silence was herself in Layla's glasses – a tired but determined woman with a sparkle in her eyes; rather than the pathetic, needy thing she felt like she was.

'It's about chosen family, Silv. Your family are either dead or not close to you. Mine aren't worth knowing. You took me in when I had nothing and you made me your family. I think you're amazing. You need to claim your babe status, rather than letting your brain – and the nobodies – make you feel like you're not enough. You are going through it right now, but you've *always* been too stubborn to ask for help, but now you have a baby and it isn't just you that you have to take care of, you can't just struggle and pretend you're ok, and my word you're finding that tough, aren't you?'

Silva flushed a beautiful shade of magenta and nodded sheepishly.

'And you know what? That's ok. The sooner you accept that that is how you feel, the better- you'll stop beating yourself up for feeling that way on top of feeling that way which ultimately makes things worse, doesn't it?'

Silva nodded again, tears in her eyes.

'I'm here to help you with that. I want you to get used to asking. The worst I can say is "no" and then you just have to find another plan. I appreciate that you're thinking of me and how much I have to do – but I will tell you if it's too much, okay? And secretly, I do like spending time with Rose. She's quite fun. And she enjoys RuPaul's Drag Race.'

'What?!'

'Ah come on, it's so colourful and full of people dancing, it's pretty much children's TV but with added gay! She thinks it's hilarious. I'm giving your baby some culture. That's what I'm for. Aunt-cle Layla teaching your baby about the broad spectrum of sexuality.'

'She is six months old!' Silva said, smirking a little.

'I'm not showing her how to put a condom on a strap-on, love, just dipping her little toes into the big rainbow of the world.'

Silva laughed. 'What is an Aunt-cle?'

'It's a term I'm trying out. It's my non-binary version of Auntie/Uncle. Although Auntie is cuter, and I'm still okay with female pronouns, but I'm trying out "they" too...that's another thing, Silva. You have never judged me for anything. Not for me disowning my family at the same time they did me, and you won't for me realising I wasn't strictly female, and you made the same joke that a good dad would have made when I told you I was pansexual, rather than ever telling me I was a weird person who sleeps with everything that moves.'

'It would be weird to treat you any other way.'

'So why do you treat yourself like you're not worthy of what you want?'

'Good question, Aunt-cle Layla.'

'Yeah, actually, "Auntie" is fine. It doesn't sound right when you say it.'

'Charming!' Silva laughed.

Layla grinned. 'Think of this, Silv, when you are tempted to be best friends with Michelle instead of me. I will only be with people who amplify my glow. Anyone else is in the way. And I want the same in return for them when they think about me. Michelle will hopefully be a great client for you, but she probably won't be a great friend.'

'Are you jealous of Michelle?'

'Absolutely not unless she's cooler than me. Which I don't think she is.'

'Nope.'

'And by the way, that mantra also works for relationships. Anyone who dulls you isn't worth having around. And wait for the one that doesn't.'

The door buzzer went, signalling food had arrived.

'Stop being so wise, Layla.'

'Only if you go get that. Please.'

Silva laughed, got up off the sofa, and spent a happy evening with her friend.

*

Silva was wiggling her body, trying to shake the nerves out. It was just *work*. Just an old friend (well, frenemy) coming in for a consultation about work. Clients were good; they stopped a young mum and her flamboyant business partner from going bankrupt.

She counted to ten, dropped her shoulders and counted five things in her eyeline. She felt calmer. Good.

'Helloooo, I've got an appointment?' Michelle's voice carried across their little office. Silva smiled in spite of herself. *She thinks there's a receptionist. Oh, Michelle.* Silva walked through to where Michelle stood and smiled.

'Welcome. Come with me, we'll sit and have a coffee. Or would you prefer a tea?'

'Green with lemon, if you have it, please' Michelle said.

Silva nodded, and settled Michelle into the consultation chairs, the ones that looked impossibly magazine-stylish and therefore should have been uncomfortable, but were like sitting on clouds, and walked into the small kitchen to dig out Eric's vast collection of tea.

When Silva returned, Michelle was already flipping through a ring binder from the table in front of her.

'This looks fantastic, Silva!' she said as Silva set down tea and a plate of biscuits.

'Thank you. Have you seen any ideas you like?'

'Loads! I love how sleek the living room is in this one. The colours... coral pink against the dark wood stain... beautiful.'

Silva blinked in surprise. None of their portfolios had that colour framing...and then she realised.

Michelle was leafing through Coral's designs.

They were expensive – and Silva instantly felt fear gnaw at her stomach. *How had Coral's designs ended up there and not in a drawer, or better yet, a sinkhole to allow the ground to swallow them whole?*

'Erm – thank you. There are loads of ideas in that one, and the other portfolios on the table. Take your time – take pictures, if you like, so you can show them to your husband. For now, let's talk about what you would like.'

'Ha! He doesn't care what his home looks like. All he wants is food on the table, a doting wife and to know that the kids missed him.'

Ugh, Silva thought. *Single parenthood is much more appealing right now.* Outwardly, she smiled brightly. 'Well, for you then. You spend a lot of time in your home. You deserve to make it beautiful for you. and obviously the children – but if you like sleek and stylish and unusual colour matches, you've come to the right place. My business partner is brilliant at that.'

'Lovely. I'm really in love with the coral and stain; I have wood flooring in the living room. This would go beautifully.'

Silva looked at her client, wondering what Eric would say. Those designs had been created exclusively for Coral on the promise that she was paying more not to have them replicated or sold to others – although she was then going to sell pictures of it to a magazine, so Silva wasn't sure if she knew people would probably have copied her.

Then again, Coral had let them down and cost them far too much.

'I think so too,' Silva said. 'I have to be honest though, that portfolio was an exclusive set for a VIP client, so I will have to ask my partner if we can use the schemes and designs.'

Michelle looked disappointed but intrigued.

'So...no one else has these designs?' she asked, her eyes lightening, intrigue taking over.

'No.'

'I would be willing to pay for the same treatment as your VIP...'

Silva studied her client and smiled. She was eating up what she had been told as though it were a deliberate sales pitch.

Maybe we should use that as a sales pitch. Silva thought, but it felt dishonest.

Michelle sipped tea and flipped through more portfolios, taking some pictures to think on and send back to Silva when she had had some thoughts.

Silva hated the next bit. She tapped her pen on her clipboard.

'What kind of budget are you working with, Michelle? You are looking at the whole house to be re-done – in stages, of course, so you can still live there?' If you go for that I would advise that you try to get out and about while it's all going on as the paint fumes and the dust from the work won't be too pleasant to be around. We will clear up – you won't know we've been there – it's just a precaution. Especially as you are pregnant.'

'You think of everything!' Michelle said, beaming. Silva flushed.

'Our labour comes to £200 a day – of course, we will try to be as fast as possible, we don't drag these things out! And we will draw your designs based on what you've liked, you get the final say and we don't start until you're happy, and the consultation fee for the whole process is 10% of the final cost. Is that okay?'

'That seems low.'

'Our main ethos is that we want to be able to give people on as many budgets as possible a beautiful home - they will get the same treatment no matter if they are a millionaire or in their overdraft. We buy the best quality we can for their money – sometimes that's my favourite bit, bargain hunting for other people – it just means the bigger your budget, the more excited

Eric gets to go round his favourite exclusive designers and buy them!'

'You make a good team, then!'

'Yes.' Silva said, realising this was the nicest conversation she had ever had with Michelle; private, no one watching, actually interested in her work rather than herself…

'I wish me and my husband were such a good team! I do everything, he would never go into business with me…'

Nice while it lasted, Silva thought.

'Ha! Eric and I aren't together… just business. I'm not his type… he's gay.'

'Oh my goodness, that explains the good taste,' Michelle laughed, 'that's embarrassing.'

'Not at all. Now, shall we talk about your budget? We can always discuss – this is just to get an idea of what you're expecting to spend and want done.'

Michelle told Silva her budget. Silva blinked a few times and her eyes watered at the figure.

'My husband makes a lot of money. This is what he has put aside.' Michelle shrugged.

'Eric is going to love you, Michelle…what does your husband DO?'

'And I love his designs. The coral. I love it… and pretty much all of the rest of the VIP portfolio.'

Silva nodded, letting the unanswered question go.

'Are you around for a bit longer? I think you and Eric should continue the discussion, you have more rooms than the portfolio did – it was a 2 bed flat, and yours is 4 bed?'

Michelle nodded. 'I have an hour before I have to relieve my mother so she can go to Pilates.'

'Brilliant. Eric should be back here shortly. Please flip through more portfolios and enjoy your tea while I give him a call.'

Silva stood and hurried out.

'Hello, my one true love?'

'Good afternoon Princess.' Silva replied. 'So. My client is

65

here. She has a huge budget for a four-bed house. She adores your brain, Eric. Trouble is, she's obsessed with Coral's portfolio – not even sure how it got there...'

'I put it there hoping for this scenario...'

'You did? Are you a bloody psychic?'

'Nah, just dumped it there and forgot.'

'Do you think we can let her use it? She wants exclusives as well.'

'My word, if she's willing to pay that and use Coral's stuff we bought in, of course she can.'

Silva breathed out happily. 'Great. Can you come back to the office and speak to her a bit – she has 2 more bedrooms and 1 more bath than Coral did. And a playroom. And an office.'

Silva could hear the delight in Eric's voice. 'On my way back now. Be there in 5. Entertain her until then... and please get the kettle on? I'm gasping.'

'I'll think about it.' Silva teased, but he had already hung up.

Silva flicked the kettle on and walked back into her little reception room, feeling happy. Michelle was happily flicking through the bigger, for-the-public portfolio.

'Eric will be here in a minute to speak to you, Michelle. I'm excited about this project.'

'Me too!' Michelle said, not looking up. Silva left her to it, made a fresh coffee and took a deep breath, the ache of tension in her shoulders feeling less, but it never really seemed to leave these days.

*

A few weeks later...

Rose was screaming her head off, teeth hurting as she had been for most of the afternoon, and poor Layla had pretty much passed her to a regular customer who had soothed her with a little finger covered in some strange remedy Silva wished she had but that was just coffee, and a distraction to Rose more than anything.

'What on earth can I do with you?!' Silva asked her screaming daughter after she refused food, bouncing, cuddles, or entertainment. Finally, her father's guitar case caught her eye and she shrugged at it. 'Nothing to lose,' she said, setting Rose down in her bouncing chair.

She pulled out the guitar and tuned it, her out-of-practice fingers remembering what to do. Rose looked at her curiously and stopped crying for a moment.

Silva strummed gently, her fingers, without her consent, playing one of her father's songs, a little three-chord ditty about letting chance take your fate.

She smiled and laughed at Rose who had stopped crying and was looking at her in stunned awe.

Silva then made up a song as she went, singing about life not going to plan and how Rose's teeth were just part of that.

'He would have loved you, kid.' Silva said when she had finished. *All of my favourite songs are about happy accidents. My whole life is a happy accident – even my job. Especially Rose. Maybe I should stop overthinking so much…as if it's that easy.*

Silva's heart soared and she kept playing to Rose, happy her daughter was finally peaceful.

She lost track of what she played after a while. Her fingers were getting sore as she heard the doorbell ring, by which point Rose was almost asleep. Silva's heart caught in her throat as she watched to make sure Rose didn't wake. She didn't. Silva set Rose's bouncer to a gentle rocking motion to keep her asleep and prepared herself to whisper a scold to Layla for forgetting her keys.

She got to the door and opened it gently with a finger to her lips. It took a second to register that who it was, and when she did, her stomach did something Olympically impressive.

It was Jake.

CHAPTER 9

Silva couldn't help herself; she spoke loudly rather than whispering.

'JAKE!'

Jake broke into a grin and her stomach went for a gold medal at somersault.

'I thought you said to be quiet?'

'Oh. Yeah. Rose is asleep,'

'I thought you were playing the guitar just now?'

'I was. It is *why* she's asleep. Erm. Come in, please come in,'

'Thank you,' he said and walked into her bathroom without asking, giving her a moment on her own.

'FUCK,' she whispered when she was sure he was out of earshot.

'Have you had dinner?' she asked when Jake came out.

'Yep. I bet you haven't.'

'I've had toast. It was all I could bother with, with a teething baby screeching the house down.'

'Ha! I've picked a bad time, then, haven't I? I can go....'

'No! Oh, sorry, I forgot to even say hello properly!' she said, giving him a huge hug, trying to inhale his scent.

'Much better,' he said, his face in her hair too. 'I missed you.'

There was a long moment where they stood like that and Silva felt heat pour through her body like liquid gold. She hadn't even known she needed it, hadn't known she was cold. Her body was torn between checking that Rose wasn't cold and staying in the hug forever.

Eventually, reluctantly, they let go of each other.

'What brings you here, Jake? And can I get you a beer?'

'I'll get it. Sit down. Stop fussing!' he said, leaving and re-appearing with a beer from the fridge. 'Your fridge is appalling, but at least you have eggs.'

'Sssh. It's been a busy week.'

'I'll forgive you. Right. I'm here to see you, and Layla, and little Rose. I'm back for Christmas and New Year, there are some clients they want me to schmooze in London so I bravely volunteered to suffer being flown back first class with very little work to do for a few weeks and to annoy you all.'

Silva punched him softly, 'it's nice to see you. Would have been nice to hear from you before though...' she said, leaning down to put her fingers gently on Rose's forehead; she felt a little cool, so she put another blanket on her.

'Sorry. Work was so busy. Good surprise, though, right?'

'Yes, of course it is.' Silva said. As she pulled herself back to the sofa – and tried to resist the urge to curl into a ball under Jake's arms – she remembered something.

'Are you seeing someone still, Jake?'

'Nah. She got bored of me. Why, are you asking?' he said, his eyes twinkling.

Heat spread through Silva once again and she felt the ache of need and longing deep within her. It would be so easy to just let go.

Silva started to say something but Layla's key turned in the door and she tried to look apologetic. *I have a seven-month-old baby. I have a business. You live on a different continent. I can't do that. But I really, really want to.*

Jake squeezed Silva's hand as if he knew, but his eyes were sad.

'Hey Layla!' Jake said, then remembered Rose and hushed his voice.

'Hey! Good to see you. Oh, Rose is asleep, well done!' Layla whispered. They walked to the sofa and kissed Jake on the cheek. They hung out together for a while until Jake yawned.

'Did you want to stay over? The sofa bed is comfy...' Layla offered. Silva wondered if she would have the strength not to invite him into her own bed if he stayed.

'Nah, but thanks. Mum made a bed for me. And I'll be snoring well into tomorrow thanks to jet lag.'

Layla nodded and hugged him goodbye. Silva did too; for a much shorter time than she had to say hello but just as fiercely.

Layla waved Jake out with Silva by her side.

'So. What did I walk in on?' Layla asked the moment Jake was in his car.

'Nothing...'

'Rubbish. You looked like a sad puppy and he looked like he was about to be neutered by a lawnmower.'

'Ha. No. just... strayed into the conversation we almost always do that hurt.'

'Ah, the old *"will-they-won't-they"*. I thought he had a partner?'

'Apparently not anymore.'

'So why can't you...?'

'Because I have Rose and work, and he lives thousands of miles away and I can't do that to myself.'

'When did you get so wise? What about just one night... I can take Rose if you tell me the witchcraft that shut her up today...'

'Ha! I played the guitar to her. No... if I want to go with Jake, I would want to do it properly. I think he's just too much of a loose cannon for that to happen now. But I appreciate the gesture.'

'OOOH. Will you play me to sleep too?' Layla asked.

'Maybe next time.' Silva said, suddenly feeling self-conscious. It was bad enough that Jake had heard her.

'You're no fun. Right. Bed. Have work tomorrow. Love you.' Layla said, jumping up and walking out.

Silva listened to the quiet for a minute before attempting to move Rose somewhere more comfortable than her chair.

She somehow managed to move her eventually without waking her up too much and ended up lying awake herself, thinking about Jake. It was going to be a long few weeks while he was here.

The next day, Silva took Rose into work and had settled her into a playpen she'd made up when Eric breezed in in silver trousers and a rainbow shirt.

'Did you dress like a sensory toy on purpose? You'll never get her off you dressed like that.'

'No, and she better not puke on these. They're label. But how can I resist cuddling this one?!'

'You simply cannot. But do not bounce her, she's full of porridge.'

Silva looked at her computer at an email that had just dropped in. She read it with her heart thudding.

'ERIC! The interior design exhibition has had an exhibitor drop out and we are first in line! Can we? It's on Saturday...'

'How much is it?'

'Errm. Discounted rate of two hundred for the day.'

'Oh, that's not bad...and the calendar is clear at the moment...why the hell not? Michelle's build starts on the following Monday, we can go out afterwards and recover Sunday...don't look like that, I want one drink out of you minimum but I'm a big boy, I can find the clubs myself...'

'Do you mean it? YES!'

'What are we going to do with madam sprog?'

'I thought we could bring her to man the stall. About time she earned her keep,' Silva said.

'I feel like she'll just poop her pants at the first opportunity,'

'Yeah, probably needs some training first. Oh well. I will sort it. Trust me,'

'Schweeet. Right. Final designs for Michelle. Let's get cracking, shall we?'

'I thought you would never ask.' Silva said and smiled.

'Layla, can I ask you an enormous favour?' Silva asked later that evening.

'You can.'

'Could you have Rose on Saturday? Eric and I have a last-minute event in London. I promise you I will buy us the best dinner ever afterwards.'

'Ah, I'm so very proud of you for asking and not hinting!'

'I know! I feel so vulnerable.'

Layla chuckled fondly. 'Yes, I can take Rose. I will ask one of the sensible staff to supervise for the day, she loves it – will help her for Christmas – and I need a day out of the shop.'

'I can pay towards that cost…'

'No, don't worry. I wanted to give her some more experience – no better way to do that than a Saturday in the run-up to Christmas!'

'Evil, but I like it.'

'I might come up to London with you and take Rose. Girl's day shopping. Or, more likely, I will take her for a walk but end up back here asleep.'

'Amazing.' Silva said, excitement bubbling in her stomach. Saturday came around fast, and Silva and Eric had worked hard to prepare, making notice boards and sharpening up portfolios for customers to view, chasing previous customers for testimonials and, of course, shopping for exhibition outfits. Silva had talked him into finally getting monogrammed t-shirts with their company details on them, and wearing them, and Eric was sulking in his shirt and black tailored jeans with Doc Martens, but only a little bit.

The day passed in a blur, and they only remembered to have a drink when Silva realised that her milk hadn't come in begging to be expressed, and they finished the day ravenous, but with thirty people having booked appointments, no business cards left, and a proud sense of achievement.

'About that drink then?' Silva asked.

'I think I'll have the one. I'm wiped. But well done, we did good.' Eric said. 'Plus, Layla might want her Saturday night to herself.'

They went to a little wine bar and clinked some expensive chardonnay, and then drove home in heavy congestion.

'Honey, I'm home!' Silva called gaily, only realising as she stepped onto her own carpet how exhausted and in need of a shower she was. She looked at the sofa and saw the outline of two adult heads.

Please do not be Jake, she thought to herself. She wasn't sure she could be near him, her resolve was low.

'Hey! How did it go?' Layla asked, pausing the TV. 'This is Opal, you know her, from the shop... she did a terrific job supervising today, so we're celebrating.' Layla said. Opal smiled at Silva in greeting. She had beautiful blue eyes, and Silva did indeed recognise her as the girl who had had trouble making latte art that didn't look phallic.

Silva caught the wild look in Layla's eye that meant they were having a very nice time indeed.

'Ah, good! Thank you again, you're both lifesavers. It went well. Is Rose okay?'

'She's perfect. The teething is still causing her aggro but she's been numbed by Calpol and I wore her out.'

'Amazing. Are you hungry...?'

'No,' Layla said, too quickly. 'We are going to the other room for a bit. If you order something...get something awesome to share, please. Thank you!' they said, pulling Opal up and out of the room. Silva smiled and rolled her eyes, trying to squash the pang of envy. 'Oh – Rose had milk at fiveish.' Layla called.

Silva looked over at Rose, who was snoozing on the sofa in blankets on cushions. Rose should be in her cot, really, but she was too happy to see Layla happy to mind that. She needed a shower so would have to move her somewhere less dangerous but for now she went to the kitchen, grabbed a bottle of water and settled down with her little girl. She turned the TV up loud enough to drown out Layla and their...employee? Girlfriend? But quiet enough to keep Rose asleep.

She realised that her life was strange.

She realised that she was mostly happy anyway.

She turned off a lovey-dovey soap storyline and turned some

soft music on instead, unable to bear to watch other people in love. (She was willing to make an exception for Layla.) She got up to put the kettle on to make a hot chocolate, in the hope it would settle her to wind down from her exciting day. She spotted Jake's traditional washing up pile still in the sink where neither she nor Layla had gotten to tackling any cleaning yet. She caught the sob in her throat before it turned into tears.

I love him and it hurts. She thought to herself. *I love him and it hurts.*

CHAPTER 10

'I want to check out Layla's café. Will you go with me?' Jake asked Silva on the phone.

'Hello to you too, Jake' Silva said.

'Sorry. Forgot to be polite for a moment.' he said, chuckling to himself, the sound of his breath against the wind outside making her stomach turn into a disco. *I've got it bad.* 'So…is that a yes?'

'Okay. When?'

'I'm client-free on the 27th? She's open then, isn't she?'

'They are, yeah,'

'Oops.' Jake said. She could almost hear his blush.

'You'll remember next time. Layla's kind enough to be open for those who want to see friends and are sick of their families post- Christmas. And works for me, our office is closed until the second so I'm just working from home, answering emails and stuff. Closing up later today.'

'It's a date, then. I'll meet you at noon,'

'Okay. Merry Christmas, Jake. Say hey to your mum for me.'

'Will do. Merry Christmas, Silv.'

They hung up and Silva drummed her fingers on her phone screen, almost calling him back and having to hang up quickly.

'Merry Christmas!' Eric sang, jingling as he walked in. Silva groaned. Rose laughed and clapped at him from her chair.

'Well, you both look VERY un-festive. Did you forget?'

'Sorry. Yeah. Madam here kept me up half the night screaming, teething, I'll put her in the pudding suit tomorrow.' Eric grinned and put Silva's coffee next to her and handed Rose a bit of flapjack he hadn't finished.

'You're an angel.' Silva said.

'No, honey. Look at the jumper. I'm Santa.'

Silva rolled her eyes and found the Muppet's Christmas Carol on her TV app for Rose to watch. She had loved Labyrinth and the Dark Crystal, so Silva decided to see if it was puppets in general that got her daughter excited or if she just liked old films. Rose clapped happily as Gonzo popped up so she figured it was probably puppets. Silva gave her a weary smile.

'They make babies cute so we forgive them for the shit, don't they?' she asked aloud.

'Oh, don't they just,' a voice she didn't recognise said. Silva blushed. She had forgotten she was at work.

'Good morning! Sorry, I thought you were my colleague.'

'No worries. It's very true. I've got two. Total nightmares, but also adorable and brilliant.'

Silva grinned in agreement. 'How can I help you today? Are we expecting you this morning?'

'No, you're not expecting me, if that's okay? I wanted to have a chat about my flat. It needs a bit of love, and my friend Michelle recommended you.'

'Ah, that's brilliant! It's better than okay! Well, you have two choices. We can either chat here and now and with The Muppets in the background and my daughter probably laughing through it or I can get you an appointment in the new year without the distraction.'

'Honestly, you don't need to worry about her! She's very sweet and if she gets fussy, I'd love to give her a cuddle. I love them at that age. *Just before* they start to really get active and then you can't get away with anything.'

'You're an absolute star. I'm Silva, my colleague is somewhere in the building,'

'Here!' Eric yelled from the kitchen.

'There he is. Let's get a drink and have a chat about what you need. What would you like to drink, er- sorry, what was your name?'

'Jean.'

'Lovely. Jean, we have tea, coffee, hot chocolate, filtered water, fruit juices… a weird selection of tea…'

'A black coffee, one sugar, please.' Jean replied.

'Perfect.' Silva said and set to work.

An hour later, Silva and Eric had helped Jean design a chic flat and they had a shopping list for antique-style furniture and quirky rugs. Jean had come back ten minutes after she had left with a huge box of chocolates and a quick hug for Rose, who had taken to Jean quite strongly half an hour into her visit when she noticed Jean's knees looked like fun to be bounced on.

'Sometimes,' Silva said as she bit into a handmade white chocolate truffle, 'I completely love my job.'

'We are very lucky, aren't we?' Eric beamed. Silva handed a bit of her truffle to an interested Rose, who managed to turn a tiny piece of chocolate into a goatee and hair accessory as well as appearing to devour it.

'Yes, we are.' Silva said. She got up from her computer to wipe Rose down and feed her in the hope she would get into her travel cot and sleep.

'I'm going to go and visit the boys out on the job and see if I can let them go home early. I'll get lunch, too. Hope she sleeps!' Eric kissed Rose goodbye and jingled his jumper at her.

Silva did not get to finish her emails. What she did get was more customers, with whom she booked appointments for the new year, and sent them away after letting them take pictures of portfolios, hoping they didn't just take them to another designer or do it themselves. On the plus side, it distracted her from constantly thinking about Jake, and Rose did sleep three hours until it was time to go home.

Eric returned just as Silva was packing up and showed her the photos of the job he'd visited.

'The boys did an *amazing* job on the flat, Silv. The customer came by as they were cleaning up and they LOVE it, they're hosting Christmas so we finished right on time.'

'Excellent.' Silva said, flipping through Eric's photos and

feeling a rush of pride.

'Let's go home for Christmas,' Eric said. 'I can't see any emails that can't wait, can you?'

'Nope.' Silva said with a grin. Eric gently took his jumper off and picked Rose up from her cot and into her pram gently while Silva shut down and tidied up a bit, locking away important things and clearing the fridge of milk, grateful that Eric was so thoughtful.

*

Christmas Day and Boxing Day passed uneventfully; no word from Jake, Layla happily loved up with Opal and texting her non-stop (Opal's family were very into Christmas and made it a 48 hour party, Layla, Eric and Silva were fond of a roast dinner and the good telly, each other's company and presents, but they were over it by 8 pm and spent Boxing day separately.)
Silva walked to the park with Rose on Boxing day, enjoying the fact she was mostly alone, enjoying letting Rose sleep and having time to relax in the cold air.

'Shouldn't you be at home with the family on a day like today?' a stranger asked her.
Silva looked at the woman who had asked her that, a sarcastic response ready on her tongue; she was used to questions from random people, often cutting about where the father was, and she had comebacks ready, but she took a deep breath instead.

'I'm just kidding, Silva! You looked like you were about to say something back.'

Silva blinked. 'Opal! So sorry - I didn't realise it was you in that hat.' Silva laughed. Opal's beautiful black hair was escaping from a woolly hat with penguins on it.

Opal grinned. 'But why are you out on Christmas? Are you escaping too?'

'Nope, just got a bit of cabin fever so I thought I'd take Rose out. We had a nice time but the flat gets so small and stuffy after a while. What about you? Are you escaping? I'm surprised you haven't been over.'
Opal shook her head, the bobble on her hat wiggling.

'I'm getting a divorce from my husband. We couldn't have kids. My family are doing my head in about it all. My mum keeps going *on and on* about it. Gran has dementia and keeps asking when her great-grandchildren are coming over. She doesn't have any. I'll see Layla tomorrow at work, we both agreed it was best to keep it family-only at Christmas. Less complicated. I wish I hadn't suggested that now.'

'That's rough. I'm sorry.'

'Thanks.' Opal replied.

'It's funny, isn't it? You would probably love the Christmas I just had, with my mum not around at all, but I would love yours. I would love a proper family Christmas just one more time. I've not had one for years and years. I used to love them. My dad would dress up as Santa, then the silliest jumper he could find, my mum would cook the most amazing dinner, my nan would tell us stories and my grandad would bring the money from his own monopoly set at home and win every year, and no one cottoned on until he died.'

'Oh, a friend Christmas would be *amazing*. No one to tell you you'll get fat if you eat any of the food THEY PUT OUT, no pressure to be social all day from wake to snooze, I bet you just sat on your phone for a bit at some points and ignored each other.'

'Yep.' Silva said and smiled.

'Bliss.'

'The modern world is a weird thing, isn't it?'

'Yes. Bring back those simpler times blokes in pubs are always on about. Actually, don't. They were probably getting away with beating their wives up and no one really cared then.' Silva said. Opal nodded her agreement.

'So, you were married?' Silva blurted out, afraid of an awkward silence.

'Yeah. He dumped me. We had enough of trying to get pregnant, I guess.'

'Forgive the intrusive question, but...'

'Pansexual. No, not as in kitchenware. Just fall in love with the person, not the gender.'

'Ha! Just checking...'

'For Layla. Yep. I understand. Anyway. That's another thing. I told my family about them and they all just think I'm having a breakdown. I've never told them about my relationships with women. They don't know how awesome Layla is.'

Silva felt a rush of warmth for Opal. 'You should come back with me. Layla would be thrilled to see you, honestly. She's – sorry, they've, I still forget sometimes - been pining to see you no matter what you both agreed.'

'I'd love that. And I have time before I have to go play nice at dinner.'

'Ha! You're making me not miss family dinners. We are having a takeaway because we're bored of Christmas food already!'

'Oh, I am too. Do you want to swap? They can pass Rose around and I can go eat your takeaway?'

'HA! No, thank you. Rose is spoilt enough at home without gaining more adoring fans. She'll become insufferable.'

*

'I've got a surprise for you!' Silva sang as she came home a little later. Layla turned round and their eyes lit up.

'It's what I've always wanted. Where did you find her?'

'She was in the park. Like a stray cat.'

Opal laughed at that.

'Opal only has an hour. Make good use of it.' Silva said, her eyes sparkling. 'I'm going to play some tunes now madam is gracing us with her consciousness.'

Rose gurgled in her pram in response.

Silva picked Rose up and left Layla and Opal to it. Rose had woken up in a good mood and so she was happy to be danced around the living room to David Bowie's greatest hits, giggling at her mother's singing.

This is what I wanted motherhood to be like, Silva thought to herself. *Amongst all the toughness and the being so skint I rely on the flat below to heat mine, I'm glad I get these moments too.*

They danced until Rose started griping with hunger, and even then, Silva danced as she mashed banana into porridge, happily not thinking about the next day or seeing Jake or anything else of worry.

*

The next morning, Rose awoke from a night of shrieking the flat down with a brightness to her that Silva thought was taking things too far. She looked in perfect health despite being on the verge of hot-enough-for-hospital all night, and Silva looked like a dishevelled wreck. Perfect to go and see Jake later.

'NO!' Silva yelled at herself as she poured boiling water into the jar of coffee instead of the mug. 'Lucky it's only got a bit left,' Silva grumbled, pouring it all into a mug and just having a very strong coffee.

After breakfast, Rose looked poorly again, and the selfish part of Silva hoped she perked up before they were due to go out. An hour later, she fell sound asleep on the sofa and Silva resisted the urge to scream and cry at her in payback for how she had been kept awake, but instead, she just followed suit.

Silva was awoken by a phone call at ten minutes to noon. Rose was also awoken and cried her head off.

'Hello?' she said to Jake after fumbling with the answer button.

'Hi, Silv. I'm running about twenty minutes late. Sorry. Is that okay?'

'Perfect actually. See you soon.' Silva said and hung up, realised the time and panicked.

It was one thing to get herself ready and out of the house in half an hour, another to get a 7-month-old sickly baby to do the same, but luckily, she looked fine upon a quick inspection and temperature test.

Panic rose in Silva's chest that she had wanted a shower, to do something nice to her hair...oh, crap was this an actual date? Hadn't she said that she couldn't do that? So why did it matter...?

Silva's heartbeat was like a marching band as she changed Rose and put her into a dress and leggings that Layla had bought her, then took her into her bedroom, put her in her walker and turned on the music and hurried to get herself ready.

A hasty use of baby-wipes and cough-inducing dry shampoo later, Silva threw on clean-ish jeans and a sparkly jumper with no signs of baby sick – or worse - on it, flicked on a tiny bit (plenty) of mascara and made her way out of the door, not sure if she felt sick from hunger or nerves.

Maybe both, she told herself.

'Hey!' Opal grinned at Silva as she pushed the pram into the café. 'what can I get you?'

'Hey.' Silva took a glance around for Jake, but he hadn't arrived yet. There were a few people sat at tables in deep conversation. 'I would love a flat white please, and a cheese panini.'

'Of course.' Opal said, raising her palm at Silva when she pulled her wallet out. 'This is on me for brightening up my Boxing Day.'

Silva smiled and thanked her.

Jake rushed in five minutes later as Silva settled into an armchair and bent to hug her.

She hoped she had put enough body spray on.

'Hey! I see you've ordered. I'll go grab something!'

'Yeah, sorry – I was hangry, I had a nap instead of breakfast.'

'No worries.' Jake said. Silva caught Rose's eye and smiled at her baby, who was making messy work of a rusk biscuit. *It's just coffee. Why am I so nervous?* She wondered. Jake returned a moment later with a teapot and cup and Silva laughed.

'What?'

'Oh, nothing, just very refined.'

'Look, I'm trying to enjoy a decent cup of tea while I'm able. They don't do it right in the States. They microwave the water, Silv. It's heinous.'

'Tough life, huh?' Silva teased.

Jake grinned. 'The toughest.' He said with a wink. Silva blushed. She shook herself and looked at Rose, who was busy noisily gumming her rusk and staring at a dog.

Silva looked up at Layla and watched them grin at customers, welcoming them, bantering with the ones who were regulars. Jake's knee brushed hers and her entire body felt electrified and she wondered if she could get him to do it again without being obvious.

You are not a teenager anymore, Silva, her unhelpful brain reminded her.

'So, how is America other than bad tea?' she asked.

Jake exhaled as Layla came to join them with a cake just for Rose on a plastic plate. Silva considered objecting based on sugar and the fate of her pretty dress but decided to leave it since Rose had seen the cake and she was happy and settled and she wanted to keep it that way after the previous evening.

'It's amazing, yeah. Really interesting work, good food, all that, but in truth it's a tiny bit lonely. I don't know many people outside of work. I miss hanging out with you two.'

Silva smiled and nodded. 'You should. We're awesome.' She said as ate the last of her panini.

'Couldn't have put it better myself.' Layla said.

They spoke for a while, Layla happily chatting to customers and getting up when their staff called them, looking happy and at home. Silva wondered how on earth they juggled that with Rose when they had her, but not for long when elderly regulars came in and greeted Rose like an old friend and she gave them huge, familiar smiles. She watched Jake as he spoke about his career. He looked happy. Professional. His teeth were much whiter than they were before, as though he had had the LA superstar treatment despite working in New York. She couldn't help but think about how her boobs were leaking milk and that she was terrified it would leak through her bra and jumper, how her business was going fine but she felt like Eric was doing all the work and she just felt...sad. This wasn't what she wanted to feel like today at all. She was with the man she loved, her best friend, and her granny-charming daughter. She should be happy.

'You're doing such a great job with her, Silva. She's gorgeous. And so happy.' Jake said, looking at Rose who was calmly watching the world around her.

'You should have seen her last night. She was a demon.' Silva said, her heart cracking a bit with sadness.

'I can't believe that,' he said to Rose, in baby-talk. She gave him a gummy smile and kicked her legs about.

'She's changed so much just since I last saw her.'

'Hasn't she just. Growing like bamboo.'

'Look at her cute little dimple!' Jake said.

'It is adorable.' Silva agreed with a little sigh. For some reason, his kindness hurt.

'Hey,' Layla said, slipping into the chair again, holding a muffin, 'so, Opal is having a New Year's Eve party at hers. Her ex moved out. They are putting the house on the market the week after and she wants to say goodbye with a bang so…let's see the year in properly, shall we? Silva. We will find someone to babysit. I will contribute if I have to SO YOU CAN COME. Please.'

'I'm in.' Jake said. He leaned back on his armchair and let his arm drape. Silva was wishing hard that it would turn into a sofa and that he would hold her with it.

'If I can get a babysitter, then one hundred per cent yes.' Silva said.

Layla held a hand up and high fived her friends in turn. Rose joined in and Layla obliged despite the sticky mess on Rose. Silva handed her a baby wipe and attacked Rose with another.

'This has been lovely, guys, but it's nearly 2 and I have to run to Prambience.' Silva said.

'What's that?' Jake asked.

'A messy baby play where they have a wonderful time and I wonder how on earth I'll get the stains out. She loves it. And it *is* quite fun. I didn't dress her correctly for that today…' Silva realised as she was talking.

'You're weird as a parent.' He laughed.

'Don't tell me you wouldn't take part in an adult one. There are paddling pools of jelly sometimes.'

'The dream.' Jake replied. Silva wrangled a screeching Rose back into her pram, said goodbye to Layla and Jake and hurried out.

In truth, she had another fifteen minutes before she had to leave but she wanted the fresh air and the noise in her head to stop before she screamed.

The proximity of Jake, of wanting what she couldn't have, hurt too much.

Maybe I shouldn't go to that party, she thought.

Much later, after Rose had been bathed and her clothes left to soak for hours in the vain hope that the messy play would wash out, Silva found some peace. She sat with her guitar, trying to wind Rose down to sleep.

She tried, but she couldn't stop thinking about Jake. She remembered kissing him first when they were seventeen because he was too scared to. She thought of the dimple in his cheek and how cute it was; the bright green of his eyes that was such a shock even when she was used to them. She had never seen anything like that colour before.

She felt a little guilty then about leaving him hanging, leaving his frantic teenage kisses unanswered. It was silly to feel that now; it was ten years ago. She had been trying to get over Joe Jenkins, a miscarried pregnancy and a future that she had thought she and Joe would have- had planned - but would never happen. Jake had come at the wrong time, but he'd opened her eyes to the possibility of love again. She just wasn't ready then.

If only it could happen now, Silva thought to herself. *But it can't. I have a child. He is working abroad. But oh he is so gorgeous and sweet and funny and...he can't even think of me like that. I'm just a mum now and he likes pristine, perfect women with no stretch marks and no baggage.* She shook her head. There was no way he had felt that same hurricane of nervous butterflies that she had today.

Rose clapped her soft pudgy hands as Silva strummed her guitar. Rose's eyes were wide and large. Silva looked closely at her daughter, and despite knowing that the worth of a girl shouldn't be in how she looks, she couldn't help but think how gorgeous a baby she was.

And then she almost dropped the guitar on her.

Rose had, somewhere along the line, in that changing-by-the-minute way, changed her eyes from Silva's blue to a beautiful green.

Rose's eyes were the exact shade of green as Jake's.

Fuck.

CHAPTER 11

'Don't look at me like that.' Silva said to Rose, who was quite innocently sitting in her bouncer watching her mother get dressed and dancing to her music. Rose chewed a toy giraffe and dribbled on herself, thinking about nothing at all. Silva shook her head. 'Really, Rose, it is perfectly natural to be nervous about this. I mean. There is no precedent. I'm not sure anything this silly has ever happened to anyone else. Having a baby with their best friend and neither of them realising. What on actual earth?' Silva babbled as she applied her makeup with shaking hands.

It had been a few days since Silva had realised Rose was Jake's baby. She hadn't seen him since, or spoken to him, managing to dodge online group chats with him and Layla by saying she had too much work to do. As she was getting ready for Opal's new year's party, everything had dawned on her at once. She couldn't hide from the truth anymore. She rubbed perfume into her wrists and behind her ears, sticking a little tiny bit behind Rose's too as she looked confused and then she laughed at the tickle of being touched behind the ears, but she liked the smell.

Later, it would help her sleep her first night without her mother. Silva didn't even list that as the reason; she just wanted her baby to remember her like this when she got older, as Silva herself did, remembering the way her mother's perfume settled into every pore of her room including the carpet and how it felt like safety, even when she was a poltergeist of a teenager storming the house.

She wondered what Rose would be like as a teenager, if she would be gentler and calmer and willing to share with Silva those steps into makeup, music and love, or if, like with her own mother, they would feel like strangers by then.

'I hope we are never strangers.' Silva said to Rose then, feeling the urge to scoop her up and cuddle her, but not daring to risk it until she had a coat on.

Rose was very good at ruining nice outfits with a well-timed vomit or sneeze.

'Right.' Silva fluffed her hair through her fingers, praying it stayed as it was; soft curls, not frizzy, held up by hairspray, hope and hair slides. 'Time to party. You have a little party yourself, little miss. Rachel is throwing a party for you and all the other kids!' Silva grabbed Rose's hands and wiggled them as one of her favourite songs came on. Rose laughed again. Silva grinned, put her coat on, and picked Rose up for a cuddle before she gently wrestled her into her car seat, and somehow carried Rose, Rose's overnight bag, her handbag and overnight clothes and herself downstairs and into the car in one shaky and dangerous manoeuvre.

'I really miss Layla.' Silva said to Rose once she had wrangled her into the car. Layla hadn't been home since Christmas, having all but moved into Opal's house. Silva felt the loss of her friend in the quiet evenings and especially after doing what she had just done on her own. What was the alternative? Make two trips and either leave Rose alone upstairs or in the car? Carry Rose up and down twice and still only have one spare hand? Rose gurgled in response. 'I haven't even told her about Jake and you yet. She's going to have a field day.'

It occurred to Silva then that the reason she felt this anxious was partly because (not that she blamed her) Layla hadn't been around to talk it over with, to call her an idiot and help her work out what to say. It scared her to think of how she would have survived her pregnancy and the first 7 months of Rose's life without them. She made a mental note to do something amazing for her friend. Silva took a deep long breath and drove Rose to Rachel's, where she was greeted by a very glittery Rachel.

'Hello, don't mind this – been making firework decorations with the toddlers.'

'Hey! Where do you get your energy from and can I *please* have some?!' Silva asked, smiling. She handed Rose over, who instantly beamed at Rachel.

'I have help. My husband loves all this. Watching them all play is far more entertaining than a usual New Year's Eve!'
Silva grinned. *This one will be fairly entertaining for me*, she thought.

Outwardly, she said, 'I bet! Text me if you need anything... I think I've told you everything. She will be hungry soonish - there are food pots in her bag, or she will probably eat whatever she is offered.'

'I'm doing mashed parsnips and swede tonight. She can have some of that. Sound nice, Rose?'
Rose gurgled in reply, still chewing her toy.

'That settles that, then,' Rachel said, 'have a brilliant night, Silva. I'll see you in the morning – 10 am latest, please.'

'Perfect, thank you so much.' Silva said and waved. Rose looked confused but didn't cry as Silva walked away and got in her car.

'Time to face the music.' Silva said to herself and drove away with a wave to Rachel's closed door.

*

'I've missed you so much! You look gorgeous!' Layla said and ran into Silva's open arms. Opal grinned at them.

'You have been away from each other for four days.' Opal said, rolling her eyes.

'It may as well have been four years. You both look stunning, too.' Silva said. 'Rose misses you, too. She keeps looking at your bedroom door when we go past it. And your spot on the sofa.'

'Bless her. Is she ok with her minder?'

'She's loving it. Didn't even blink at being left – she'll be fine. It was me that had to stop myself crying!'

'Ha! You're a right softie since you spawned.' Layla said.

Silva grinned. 'Rude. But true. So...drinks? The house looks awesome, guys.'

And it did. Paper chains in every colour adorned the walls, as well as the tasteful Christmas decorations, tasselled banners saying 'Happy New Year', and there was a table full of alcohol and food.

'I was meant to come round to help!' Silva protested.

'Yeah, we beat you to it. More drinking time!' Opal said. 'I'm going to make us a cocktail.'

A few delicious, but lethally alcoholic cocktails later, and just before guests began to arrive, Silva waited until Opal got up to refill glasses before she spoke to Layla.

'I need to tell you something, La-la.'

Layla grabbed Silva's face in their hands. 'Go on then, my pretty.'

Silva took Layla's hands and held them.

'Rose is Jake's.'

Layla's mouth fell cartoon-open.

'WHAT?!'

'I know. He doesn't know yet. I'm going to talk to him tonight. But her eyes have changed, Layla. Bright green. His green.' Silva said, the nerves in her stomach holding a disco but she felt glad to tell someone.

'You – on that night – when? What? I didn't see you – what?!'

'I know. We were *so* drunk and no matter what I do I can't remember who it was. Just that it happened and was over with and oh my goodness I wished that I had known so much sooner.'

'I don't.' Layla said, their face changing from shock to happiness to confusion and back to shock. 'This has been the best possible thing for you. You look amazing. Healthy. Happy. Having her has made you blossom – you're looking after yourself, because you have to for her, but I think you would now anyway? You are so much more...grounded. And I think it would have been less of a revelation if you had Jake with you the whole way. I mean, it's so cool that he's her dad. And you know that he would do anything for you and he will support you and she's at a good age to get him involved but... this was about you, y'know?'

'This is why I need you with me at all times. You make things make sense. You make me feel better.'

'I just point out what is staring you in the face, babe. I'm so excited for you!'

Opal came in with their drinks. 'What did I miss?'

'Tell you later, babe. It's going to be epic though.'

'Okay.' The doorbell rang just as Opal went to sit down, and she and Layla got up to start greeting guests.

Jake walked in not long after, hair slicked back into a quiff, the gel in it making his brown hair look darker. Silva instantly thought of him as a teenager, with his leather jackets and his not-caring-to-be-cool Grease styling. She had loved him, then. But she was in the clutches of heartbreak, grief, and still dealing secretly with a miscarriage she wasn't mature enough to understand. It wasn't the right time then. Could it be now?

*He lives and works abroad…*Silva's rational side reminded her. Her mouth went dry. She sipped her cocktail.

Jake looked around the living room which was already getting cramped and his face lit up when he saw Silva in an unstoppable smile. She couldn't help smiling back at him.

'What are you drinking?' Jake asked her as he bent to hug her.

'Some concoction of Opal's. It's nice. Want one?'

'Of course I do. Where can I find one?'

'Kitchen. I think she made up a pitcher. I'll get you one.'

'Don't worry – I'll go. You look hot tonight.' Jake said before he strode to the kitchen. Silva felt her cheeks burn. It was nice to be wearing clothes that made her feel like her old self. She recognised the feeling of accidental neglect – of spending her life in clothes with faded patterns and holes in them, and not prioritising herself and felt suddenly defensive. *That is the mum life*, she thought to herself. I'm not the most important person now. *I'm still important.* The other part of her brain countered. *Enjoy this. Worry about the rest later,* Silva thought.

When Jake came back in with drinks and a bottle of tequila in the crook of his arm, Silva took in his outfit; black jeans, a black tee, and a shimmery gold blazer.

'You're drinking like you mean it already,' she said.

'Of course. Don't get to see you out on the town much these days. Making the most of it.'

Silva resisted the urge to leave, fetch Rose, and go home where it was safe and her body didn't have to feel like it was having a hurricane rage through it with how close he was. His warm leg was touching hers, as they tried to leave enough space on the enormous sofa for other guests (Silva wondered how Opal had afforded this, given she worked as a barista, and then she stopped wondering; Jake had brushed his foot against hers and nothing else mattered.)

'In that case, let's party. I feel like Layla will be socialising all night, though.'

'We'll get her dancing in a short while…when was the last time we did this?'

Silva's stomach lurched. *If I'm right, then that would be the night you got me pregnant.*

'Erm. Probably our big night out we had to celebrate our lives going well. You going to America. Me with the business. Layla with the coffee shop.' Silva said after a faux-thoughtful pause.

'Yes! I think that's right. That was a heavy one. Messy.'

'I don't even remember much.'

'Nor me. The hangover was the *worst.*'

Mine was the best, Silva thought.

'Did you pull that night?' she asked, heart in her throat.

'Well, you certainly did,' he teased. 'You got the best souvenir of all,'

'That's my kid you're talking about. She isn't a fridge magnet.'

'I know. I'm sorry. I was trying to compliment you. She's a cute kid,' he said, backing his knees off from hers a little.

'Did you get a souvenir?' Silva asked, feeling a chill.

'This scar,' he lifted his shirt to reveal a two-inch scar on his hip.

'How?'

'Fell off the podium onto a bit of glass. Didn't even know it happened until it hurt the next day and I got a nurse to pull the glass out.'

'Idiot.' She touched the scar tissue softly and he shifted a little at how cold her fingers were. She looked at him, resisting the magnetic urge to kiss his lips. It seemed so easy to just let go and kiss him, but he'd deflected her original question. And she was terrified of bringing it up, but she had to. He deserved to know. Even if it ruined their friendship and the current of energy between them, it wasn't fair on him or Rose not to tell him.

'We need more drinks before I can deal with tequila,' she said, tapping their empty glasses. She had a plan. She got up and sashayed to the drinks table, nodding and exchanging "hello" with as much tipsy grace as she could muster to familiar faces from the café. She poured a cocktail of spirits and juice in random measures – the pitcher Opal had made was already empty – then walked back to the sofa. His eyes were on her, already a little drunk, she could tell from his lazy smile. She handed him his drink. He sipped and laughed, then she did the same. They held their noses, grimacing, and necked half each. 'What did you put in this, Silv?'

'Whatever I found!'

'I don't know how you've done this but it's horrible...with an amazing aftertaste.'

'I think you'll find that is a skill, not an accident' she laughed.

Silva checked the clock on the wall; somehow it was already 8 pm. She felt like Cinderella, her time away from normal life measured carefully.

Layla sidled up to them, taking care that they weren't interrupting anything.

'My pretties,' they slurred. 'Do you think it is time to dance?'

'Turn the music up, Layla. Let's dance!'

Jake and Silva took hearty swigs of tequila and shuddered the alcohol away in the time it took Layla to find their playlist and turn it all up, loud.

They were pretty drunk. Not so drunk that they wouldn't remember – no, Silva wouldn't do that again, but drunk enough that dancing was a good idea. Jake stood up carefully and helped Silva. They leant on each other when the ground swayed underneath them.

Somehow, they helped Layla move the sofa out of the way, and the coffee table, and then they began to dance. Slowly but surely, almost everyone at the party danced – other than those who didn't want to, who kept to the hallway, the kitchen and in some cases, the bedrooms.

'Silva,' Jake said in Silva's ear as they danced, closer and closer. They had been dancing for hours, stopping only to refill glasses or chat to people.

'Jake,' Silva said as a slow song came on. Jake spied Layla fiddling with the playlist to make that happen and he winked at her across the room.

'I don't have someone to kiss for New Year's,' he said.

'I'll be your kiss.' Silva said back. Confidently, cheekily. Sounding like someone she had been ten years ago.

'You will? I don't want to complicate... you said it was a bad time.'

Silva looked around. 'It's New Year's Eve. Everyone kisses everyone. Don't they? It *is* a bad time. But it's just a kiss. To say happy new year, I miss you.'

'Deal.' he said. He smiled at her and took her by the waist to dance slow. She didn't resist.

When the song finished, he released her gently.

'It's too hot.'

'Agreed.' Silva said, although she would have been happy to be held by him even if she was on fire. 'Where are you going?'

'Toilet.' Jake said.

'Be back before midnight,' she replied.

'Can't promise anything,' he said, staggering off. It was

11.15 pm. A round of premature fireworks had gone off outside, and a wave of party poppers. Silva was going to kiss Jake and it was fine, it's what you did on New Year's Eve. It felt weird to have planned it, like little kids and adults all at once. Her stomach felt like it was having its own fireworks display and it didn't stop when Jake came back and the sight of him made her body tingle. She grabbed his hand and they danced some more.

'Shall we sit down for five minutes?' Jake asked. 'I am getting too old to dance all night.'

'You wait 'til the hangover kicks in. We'll be fighting it off until February.' Silva replied as they walked to the unoccupied sofa.

Jake chuckled. 'It's worth it.' He sat down and opened his arms for a cuddle. Silva settled into his armpit and they watched people dance, drink, chatter and kiss for a comfortable five minutes while everything spun, and she tried to ignore her heart using her ribcage as its drumsticks in a heavy metal beat.

'You never answered, Jake.' Silva said after a few minutes of peace between them.

'Hmm?'

'Did you pull the night I got pregnant and you got a scar?' she asked, hating to break a perfect moment.

'Yes,' he said softly. Her stomach lurched.

'Who?'

'Want the full or the short story?' he asked. She stretched her leg out.

'Since I'm comfortable...'

'Once upon a time...all right, fine,' he said as she tickled his ribs. 'That night, we were ALL wasted, right? After we'd done our bit on the podiums, we were drunk enough to sink a ship.'

'We were the Smirnoff Iceberg the Titanic is afraid of.'

'Yeah.'

'You do know that club doesn't have podiums, right? They were tables.'

'I know. I noticed the next time I went and the landlord recognised me and told me off.' He said, biting his lip with mock shame.

'Oops.' Silva giggled.

He was toying with a bit of her hair, making the curls spring out and bounce back. She didn't mind; it wasn't the perfect 'do she had left her flat with but hours of dancing tended to do that.

'There are blank points between getting from the dance floor to being in the toilets, doing *it*,' he said, kind of childishly. 'And then another gap between that and throwing up outside before Layla and I got a cab home. We had no idea where you were but you seemed okay when you eventually picked up your phone. So yes, I pulled, but no idea who.'

'And what was the short version of that?'

He shrugged. 'I had sex with a girl in the women's *convenience*.'

'That's a beautiful story.' Silva looked at him levelly, the pupils of his eyes like tiny dots, his lovely hair floppy again thanks to him playing with it.

'Why do you want to know so badly, anyway?'

'What?'

'Why is it so fascinating to you? It's not news when I act like that, is it? It was ages ago.' he said.

'Did it occur to you I might have a reason to be interested?' she said, chest puffed with fear.

His face drained of colour. 'No,' he lied.

'Jake,' She whispered in his ear. 'Come outside with me. Just for a minute.' She thought she might have a heart attack, but she'd started being brave. Why stop now? 'It's almost midnight. Come and sit in the garden?'

The living room bay window overlooked the garden but at least it was quieter and she wouldn't have to shout and chance that in between songs the whole party would hear their story.

'Okay.' he said and she took his hand.

'You still have five minutes before countdown!' someone yelled amidst the wolf whistles as we left.

Outside, the throb of the music was dulled a little and the cold was blissful.

'Silva,' Jake said. He was shaking, although if it was nerves as well as cold, she couldn't tell. She pushed his hair back from his face.

'Jake. Please. Try and think about this. Was that us? Did we have sex that night?' she asked, then laughed, because she was drunk and high from the scent of him, and also because she'd never asked anyone something so ridiculous.

'I think we did,' he replied. There. That was it. She looked deep into his bright, emerald-green eyes and they were sharp behind the alcohol. She felt queasy with the truth of it, the finality of knowing.

'Fuck,' he said. Silva nodded, tears in her eyes.

'I know, right' she clasped him in a vice of a hug and the tears rolled down her cheeks.

'When did you realise?' he asked, letting go gently.

'The other day. After coffee. Rose has your AMAZING eyes. And your dimple, but I thought that was a baby thing until I saw her eye colour had changed.'

'I don't have a dimple,'

'Yes, you do,'

'Do not.'

'Do too.' She carried on, but he was laughing. She poked her finger into his dimple.

'Oh.' he said.

'When did you realise?'

'Same day as you. She has Mum's eyes, Silv. It took a while to realise it, but they're the same colour. Well, same as mine too, I guess. But yeah. You're right. They changed from just before Christmas to then.'

'Shit.'

'Yep.'

There was a silence between them in which they, shaking and shaken, just looked at each other.

'What do we do now?' Jake asked as the music inside came to a halt and the TV commentary was turned up loud, and the patio door opened.

Silva took a deep breath. 10 seconds. 'We have a brand-new year to work that out.'

'*9!*' came the chorus around them.

'Fresh start?'

'*8!*'

'Yes.'

'*7!*' They embraced, hearts beating against each other, clear and hard and loud.

'*6...*'

'To new beginnings,' Jake said.

'*5...*'

'I don't have a drink to toast,' Silva said.

'*4...*'

'Me neither...'

'*3!*'

'Ah, screw it,' Jake said, pulling her closer.

'*2....1!*'

He dipped his head and they kissed, urgently and passionately, as the New Year fireworks exploded. Too hard for a chaste New Year kiss, which is what Silva had signed up for, too gentle for what she *really* wanted. But for the moment, for what had just happened, it was perfect. When they came up for air, the world felt changed.

'Happy New Year,' Silva whispered.

'Happy New Year.' he pressed his forehead against hers. Fireworks illuminated purple and green and pink in Jake's hair and lit up his eyes. Helpless, they kissed again, her heart pounding, and this time she allowed herself to remember the last time they'd kissed like this. They had been teenagers, desperately sad and dramatic and wanting each other but something was in the way. Well, to be fair it had actually been about eighteen months ago, they just didn't remember it.

Reluctantly, she pulled away first, trying to ignore the sobering stabs of guilt pitched against the urge to never stop. It was right and wrong all at once; perfect and forbidden, bliss and torture.

'I need another drink.' Silva said. Jake sighed into her

shoulder. She tried her hardest to ignore how she wanted just to let go and scratch the itch that was deep inside of her; she could feel him against her and knew how easy it would be, just four layers of fabric separating them. He dropped a flutter of kisses on her cheeks, cleaning the tears away. She felt herself begin to sway. No. *He lives in another country. You are setting yourself up for pain.*

'We should go back inside now.' She said, not wanting to stop, but not wanting to regret going too far.

'Mmmm.'

'Jake, this is important. We can't just do this. Much as I'd *like* to, there are things we have to talk about first. We have a child, Jake,' she said, pushing her head against his to stop him nuzzling and make him pay attention.

'We're parents.' Jake said, eyes growing wide as the reality settled on him. 'Oh, wow.'

'So maybe we should cool it on the lusty side until we fig- ure out what we're going to do'

'Sober?' Jake asked. 'I promise not to do a runner.' he said. He made them drinks as Silva's hands were shaking too much. He put a small amount of alcohol in, some sensible part of him knowing losing the next day would be a waste of the few he had left in England.

'Intense.' Silva heard someone say, a snapshot of a conver- sation about her and Jake. She looked up and saw Layla telling someone to shut up. Silva sent Layla a smile across the room and nodded when Layla raised a questioning thumb at her with raised eyebrows.

Silva turned to Jake.

'Yes, sober. I have to get Rose quite early tomorrow but we can talk in the evening? Or I'll call you when she goes to sleep? Are you working?'

'No work tomorrow. Just a roast at my mum's... I'll bring you some if you like. I'm cooking it.'

'That would be amazing. Yeah. Come over. For now...let's enjoy the party. For what is left of it?'

'Plan.' Jake said. Layla came over, very drunk.

'I'm sorry guys, I was barely with you. I love you.' Layla said.

'You danced with us for like two hours.' Silva replied.

'Oh. Did I? Good. Thank you for coming – isn't Opal fantastic? I love her. Best employee ever. Don't tell the others. Oh, shit they are all here. YOU'RE ALL THE BEST EMPLOYEES I COULD ASK FOR. I LOVE YOU ALL. BUT OPAL MORE. SORRY.'

'Oh, Layla. I got someone pregnant in a nightclub toilet and didn't know and yet I'm still cringing for you.'

'We're joking about this already?' Silva asked

'FUCK! Rose?' Layla yelled.

'It's ok, Layla, we've had the conversation.' Silva grinned. She looked at Jake. 'I'm sorry I told her first.'
Jake smiled and shook his head helplessly in response.
Opal came over and held a swaying Layla up.

'People are starting to leave. Shall we say goodbye?' she said. 'I think you need to go to bed.'

'NO BED! PARTY!' Layla said, then had to cover their mouth as they stifled a retch.

'Exactly my point. Come on. Say bye and thank you. Guys, the spare room is ready for you. I can't guarantee it's as clean as it was earlier but it smelt fine a minute ago.'

'Nice.' Silva said, laughing. She kissed Layla on the cheek. 'We can start clearing up.' she said to Opal.

'No, no, that is for tomorrow. For now, eat. Drink. Talk. Dance until I have to turn off the music for the neighbours' sake. Enjoy. It's been nice to see this house filled with joy again.' Opal said with a sad smile. Silva hugged the half of her not propping up Layla.
Silva looked around the living room. The party was indeed beginning to dwindle already, people who an hour ago had thrown themselves around were looking queasy and gingerly putting on their coats, seeking out Opal to say goodbye.
A few people remained on sofas happily with drinks and cheerful expressions. The music had been turned down to a sensible

volume.

It was time to talk.

Jake gestured his head towards the stairs.

If this was a movie, this would be the happy ending. Cut to credits. Viewer, she found him, they are in love. The end. Silva thought. But it wasn't. Her head was a mess and the only thing she held on to in that moment was that he hadn't run away from her screaming.

In fact, quite the opposite, and had there not been a Rose to complicate things, she might have considered something drunk at a party with him before he went off and oh - that is exactly how she had gotten into this pickle the first time.

They reached the spare room and went inside. Opal had left them a bottle of water on each side of the bed.

The air hung with the aroma of burnt party poppers. Silva didn't know what to say. She wanted so badly to just grab him and kiss him, and never stop, but there were more important things to sort out. They looked at each other, minds scattered like dandelion seeds in high winds.

Silva swayed a little with the alcohol.

'Jake, you know you don't – I'm not going to pressure you or force you - but I want her to know you. As in, who you are, okay?'

'Of course,' Jake's solemn reply came.

'But you don't have to be part of this if you don't want to. I don't want money or anything, no pressure-just be there if she wants you, right?'

'Silv, don't be so silly. She's my daughter. My goodness, I wish we'd known so long ago.' He pulled off his top. Silva's stomach gave a lustful lurch as though there was something inside her propelling her towards him.

'Let's talk tomorrow, Silv. Just relax for now.' Jake said. Silva unhooked her bra without taking her eyes off him.

'You can't sleep in that dress - thing. It'll be so uncomfortable. Here,' he said, handing her his discarded shirt. 'Have this.'

'Close your eyes.' Silva said, pulling her dress off slowly, with no idea if he was watching her. Hoping he wasn't. Wishing he was. She pulled his top on, inhaling the scents that it carried including her perfume.

She didn't want to tell him she had brought pyjamas. They weren't exactly anything to show off about, and she was intoxicated by the smell of his tee. Of course, he hadn't brought an overnight bag. *He is not ready for this.* Silva thought with a pang. *For what? You just said you haven't drawn up a contract or anything. Chill your boots, Silva Jones,* she sighed.

'Fuck, Silv. I live with my *mum*. I have nothing to offer you.'

'Sssh. There's a lot to go through tomorrow. You only live with her because you work away. And there's no shame in living with your mum. If my mum had stayed here, and we got on, we would probably still live together too. It's not that unusual, Jake. Let's try to get some sleep, maybe?'

Silva clicked the light off as he bent to turn the lamp on. She slipped into the bed as modestly as she could, given she was wearing a thong and a tee-shirt not designed for boobs.

'No funny business,' she said, though she kind of wanted him to try. He pulled the thick duvet over them, and switched off the lamp, then hooked his arm around her waist. For two people not going too far, they were crushed close together as though they needed to be.

Silva's heart rate was still high. Jake's brain felt like an overloaded circuit. Silva's thoughts raced; the room swayed a little with the new position of her body. She tried not to think about what all of this was and what it meant; instead tried to think about what she was going to look like when she took her makeup off in the morning. She didn't even want to think about her hair, but, she supposed, with a smile into the darkness, Jake's warm body behind her, that hair and makeup like that felt like a waste to be gently wiped off and let loose, rather than sweat off in dancing, or hair coming loose from hands running through it or touching it, the urgent pull to be close…

Silva tried her best to blink that thought away too and tried to sleep.

Jake waited until he felt her body relax and her breathing go even before he allowed himself to relax too.

'I love you.' he whispered to her back, his entire being a mess of lust and confusion and alcohol, but somehow despite all of this in their minds, and the music still thumping, they fell asleep.

Tomorrow was a new day.

CHAPTER 12

Silva woke before Jake, a shudder to her system that had expected to be woken up hours ago by a hungry baby. It took a moment for her eyes to adjust to the unfamiliar furniture around her and the feeling of a warm arm clutching her.

'Oh.' Silva said, as it all dawned on her. She checked her phone for the time. 8 am. There was still plenty of time before she had to get Rose, and she needed it. The room still span. Perhaps she would walk to fetch her daughter.

Jake stretched next to her, his body clicking. He yawned. He jerked backwards in surprise.

'Erm, good morning, Silv,'

'Morning, Jake,' Silva said, suppressing a giggle.

'Did you sleep okay?'

'Yeah. I haven't been cuddled all night in AGES. It was nice.'

'Oh, shit, sorry. Did I overstep?'

'No. I mean. It doesn't fall into the definition of "funny business". It's okay.'

Jake blew out a relieved sigh. Silva rolled over, smiling. It did not help to bring down his morning glory that she looked beautiful, even with bed hair and smudged make-up.

Think neutral thoughts, Jake, he thought.

Silva caught the look on his face and understood. They wanted each other. He wanted her even though she must look like a total mess, having not worried about make-up remover, tying her hair up or even brushing her teeth.

Yikes.

But, she thought to herself, *he was also about as fresh as a dead daisy and she was resisting hard the urge to fill the air space between them.*

It would be so easy. To kiss him. To lose herself there. She knew he wanted her, too.

But it wasn't just about her or him. It was about Rose, too.

But surely, just one kiss wouldn't hurt...was what Silva thought as Jake pulled her close to him and their lips met and they both felt it, the magnets within them meeting their release, and they kissed urgently for a minute until she stopped and pulled away.

'I'm sorry.' Jake said. He kissed her on the forehead and shuffled out of bed.

'Don't be sorry for finding me irresistible.' Silva said as she grinned, her heart pounding. Jake laughed and left the room, turned away from her like a schoolboy hiding his erection in a lesson.

Silva took a deep breath and several sips of water from the bottle on the bedside table, then dug out some make-up wipes and set to work on her face.

It wasn't as bad as it could have been, she thought as she looked in the mirror, but whether that was because her eyes were glassy with post-kiss lust or that she was possibly still a bit tipsy, she didn't know.

'Sensible adult mode, Jones.' she said to herself.

'Yep. Take it you didn't shag then?' Layla said, coming into the bedroom.

'Somehow managed not to.' Silva said with a laugh that came out more like a sob.

'Oh, honey. You'll work through this. Just try to keep it in your trousers until you have, no matter how big his puppy-dog eyes are or how romantic it is. He has to leave the country in a few days.'

It hit Silva in the gut to remember that part.

'Yes, you're right. How are you feeling, La-la?'

'Like I got hit by a bus carrying seventy-five tons of bricks. No regrets, though. There's no way I'm opening the shop until later. Once you go I'm going back to bed.'

'You can go now, Layla. We'll see ourselves out.'

Layla's eyes lit up. 'Keep me in the loop.' they said, kissing Silva on the cheek with boozy breath and marching back to bed.

Silva decided to make use of a shower in which she didn't have to factor in Rose, and when Jake returned in last night's clothes she ventured in, helping herself to a beautifully soft towel from the airing cupboard, which was loaded with them.

Silva's towels were all rougher than beard stubble – Rose had her own soft baby towels. Looking around at Opal's lovely – if lacking in personality – home, Silva thought about how she spent her working life decorating for others, designing them wonderful things, but her own flat was hand-me-downs, bargains or ancient things. Her favourite mug was from a charity shop and boasted that she was the "world's best grandad". She had cushions on the sofa from an old job in a print shop, emblazoned with images of someone else's family from where they had rejected the print quality, although it was totally fine. She knew every whisker of the front view of a stranger's Cocker Spaniel.

In short, she thought as she stepped under the hot shower with no one screaming or babbling to worry about, the flat could do with a make-over. Health visitors had been happy enough with the hygiene, the covered plug sockets, and Rose's tiny room being warm enough (and they had enjoyed the unicorn mural that Silva had painted, too. Silva had handed them business cards in a rare moment of boldness.) Layla's room was a gentle yellow with mauve soft furnishings which shouldn't have gone together but it really did.

Silva's was magnolia, with once-red bed sheets from 2006.

She made a note to update that as she washed her hair, enjoying the removal of the styling products and the smell of smoke.

A little while later she emerged, clean and dressed, and went back to her room, a knot in her stomach wondering if Jake had left. What it would mean if he had, without a goodbye or a note and what she would do.

She needn't have worried. He was sat on the bed, scrolling on his phone. He smiled when he saw her.

'Croissant? Opal dropped you one in.'

Silva nodded and sat cross-legged eating it on the bed.

Jake had a flashback to her being seventeen, on her childhood bed, picking carefully at a sandwich as he watched her, trying to get her to eat *something.* Times had changed, he thought, as she picked crumbs up with her finger and ate them.

'What?' she asked.

'Nothing,' he shook himself and gave her a hug. 'Check out the pictures from last night, Silv. We cut some serious shapes.'

Silva looked and laughed with him. She checked the time on the screen.

'I have to go get Rose. Erm. You have your roast today. Can you come over afterwards?'

'Yeah. I'll bring food with me.'

'Thanks.' Silva said. She kissed him on the cheek.

They both got up but Silva beat him to the door, grabbed her bag and was gone. She stopped to thank Opal and say goodbye and then left to collect her daughter, for whom nothing had changed other than a newfound liking for mashed swede.

*

Later, Silva paced her flat as she tried to get Rose to nap. Her hangover was still with her, and she suspected it would be for at least another day. The older she got, the worse the hangovers were. Finally, she sat on her tired sofa, the cushion slack with age but soft. She looked at the walls, wondering what colour to paint them – she wasn't fond of wallpapering – and started thinking about what colour Jake would like; about moving him in here, the three of them being a little family.

And then she remembered that he lived and worked on a different continent.

The door buzzer went. Silva picked it up and Rose stirred. Silva pressed the buzzer to let Jake in and rocked Rose, trying to get her back into her drowsy state. It would be easier if she only had to worry about this conversation and not her as well, but it would have to be a case of come what may if not.

Her stomach twitched with nerves. Jake came in, having

changed – thankfully – into clean clothes. Blue jeans and a faded Star Trek t-shirt.

He handed her a plate of food, which she put in the fridge for later and flipped the kettle on. Rose looked alert and interested. Jake's voice had woken her properly and Silva gave up hope of getting her to nap; she handed her to Jake and they sat down.

Jake's face was different when he was with Rose; before, he approached her like a fun uncle, trying to make her laugh. Now, he looked at her with awe on his face.

Silva almost made a joke about that face disappearing once he changed her nappies but held her tongue. He needed to have this moment. She thought of the pregnancy he could have shared with her, helped her through, been excited by. She felt the loss slam against her chest.

But she blinked through it; there was nothing she could do about the past and besides, Layla had pointed out how good it had been for her.

Father and daughter stared each other out until Jake poked his tongue out at her and Rose copied him.

'How do you feel?' Silva asked.

'Like I'm on an emotional rollercoaster. Like I'm falling in love but want to be sick. How are you meant to feel?'

'Pretty much how I felt too when I held her for the first time. You seem to be on the right track.' Silva laughed.

'You did all of that alone...bloody hell.'

'I had Layla. I had you in spirit. This wasn't your life, though. I understand. You were so brilliant when you met her first time though. No one thinks to bring easy food. It's all flowers and chocolate, more admin to look after the flowers and I couldn't eat chocolate all day unless I wanted scurvy.'

Jake smiled. 'I was worried you wouldn't eat enough.'

'I do now. Things changed when I found out I was pregnant. I suddenly remembered I deserved to live and be fed. She prompted it – I needed to – but I wanted to, too. I'm sorry I worried you.'

'What made you decide to keep her?'

'It's hard to pinpoint. The right answer is that I wanted to raise a child into an adult and all of that. But it's a bit more nuanced, I guess. I wanted to prove that I could be a good parent. I wanted to care about something, I think? It was terrible timing. I had just left a job to start a business, but I didn't know if I would get the chance to do it again – and I am stubborn and I isolate myself, I know, don't give me that look. I looked for her father. I went to the club and asked for CCTV. In every bloke I've walked past for months I've been searching for similarities to her or any memories of a face. And there you were all along, waiting in her eyes. In her ears. Maybe her chin.'

'Yeah, that's my cute chin all right,' Jake said, tickling Rose under hers. 'She is quite calm about who she goes to, isn't she?'

'She trusts my instincts.'

'Clever baby.'

'Yeah. What did you think when you found out about her?'

'I was scared you would change. Become like…a mum. You know, only ever talk about her poo and lose who you are but you didn't. You're you, just softer. Kinder to yourself. You are happy. You just seem natural with her. And it all feels so surreal.'

'Take a minute. It's a lot to freak out about.'

'I'm ok. I just – what kind of dad do I want to be? What kind of dad do you want me to be? I have no point of reference other than the occasional e-mail. It's all such a shock.'

'You have to decide to be your own kind of parent. I miss my dad but I didn't always get on with him. It's easy to mis-remember him since he is dead, to rose-tint his whole life as basically everyone did. It's like people are so obsessed with the idea that death redeems you that they forget that…what you did in your life still has an impact. I remember going on cute Sunday runs and bike rides with him, but what people don't remember or didn't see was his obsession with getting faster. With personal bests. With never having a tiny bit of fat on our bodies. We forget the ways he fucked me up and just focus on the success – people are not perfect. I know that you didn't have a father figure in your life and I was lucky but – as I say, you have to decide to be your own kind of parent. Ideally, one that doesn't inspire your child to get herself an eating disorder that, ten years after your death, she only just begins to recover from and even then, only because she had a child and learned about real, good food.' Silva said thoughtfully, stroking her stomach. 'A father who works *with* me for what is best for her, even if we hate each other sometimes.'

'I can't imagine hating you.'

'I know, but things might get tough.' Silva shrugged.

Rose let out a soft snore, having fallen asleep in Jake's arms. Silva passed him her blanket.

'Looking like you're doing good so far, Jake,' she said. 'We can put her in her cot and chat more.'

'Give me a minute?'

'Okay. I'll go heat that food up.'

Silva left them to it, her heart filling up.

When she came back, Jake was just staring down at her.

'I feel like I've been slapped around the face and won the lottery.'

'Why slapped?'

'Just… the shock? Silv, how did we get so drunk we didn't remember?'

'I don't know. I don't even remember so much as kissing you that night. But I remember holding someone's hand and dragging them in there. I had hoped if we ever got together, I would at least remember it.'

'I don't think it lasted long enough to remember it. But I agree with you. It shouldn't have been like that.'

Low in Silva's stomach she felt herself respond. No – not the time for that. She ate a roast potato.

'Can't change it now. But next – if there is a next time, it'll be sober.' Jake said.

Silva bit her lip. 'Do you want a next time?' she asked, her whole body seeming to be subject to the answer.

Jake flushed, 'yes. You know I do. Do you?'

'Yes, Jake. I do.'

'So... when?' Jake said, half laughing, not joking.

Silva grinned and put her plate to the side and said, 'we've got things to talk over first. Keep it in our pants for now, can't afford another one quite yet.'

'I have cond...oh, you're joking,' Jake said and shook his head. 'Shall we put her to bed, then?'

Silva nodded and Jake got up. She showed him the cot and how to put her in it safely, switched the baby monitor on and left Rose to sleep.

In the living room, they sat down.

'I feel like I'm negotiating a peace treaty.' Jake said.

'You're an idiot.' Silva said, laughing. 'No. we just need to figure this out. This is for Rose. She deserves to know who you are and what to expect from you – too many kids don't get what they're expecting from their parents. As you well know.'

'Yeah. Obviously I want to be in her life – your life – all of us, together. Silv, I love you. I want us to be together.'

'I want that too but – what if we split up? Would you still want to be in her life?'

'Yes.'

'Okay. I don't want to pressure you but we are running out of time before you go again. The finer details will come to us, I'm sure. This won't be easy, you know that right?'

'I know that. Silv. Stop looking so serious at me. We've got this. I'm excited. Scared, but excited.'

Silva took a deep breath. 'I hope so but - there's an elephant in the room.'

'My contract for work finishes in May. I'm coming home then.'

'Well, that. But also. You're going to need to start telling people. Your whole life is about to change, Jake.'

'Oh. I've just realised what you mean.'

'Go on.'

'I have to tell my mother.'

Silva grinned at Jake's pale face and said, 'yes.'

CHAPTER 13

'When should we do it?' Jake asked.

'The question is also – how? Do you want us to be there too – how is her heart? I don't want you to give her a big shock if she's not well.'

'Fine as far as I know…you have to tell *your* mum, too, Silv.'

'My mum isn't as involved with my life as yours is. I'll tell her next time she phones me.'

'Show off. Erm. I'll tell her on my own – then see if she's happy to see you both?'

'She'll be thrilled. Surprise Grandbaby? Yes please! It'll be like having a mini-Jake to coo over while real Jake is in America.' Jake winced at the reminder that he had a real-life job to go back to.

'Which means I should do this today.'

'Agreed.'

'But I don't want to leave you – this.'

'Okay. But you need to go before she goes to bed. And we can arrange to go over tomorrow.'

'Yes, you have yourself a deal.'

'Good.'

They sat a moment.

'So, now what? The baby's asleep and all I want to do…'

Silva took a deep breath and said, 'I know, Jake.'

'I can't go back to work.'

'You have to.'

'Aren't you meant to romantically beg me not to?'

'Jake…of course I don't want you to go. This isn't great timing, but we have time. We have her whole life. I love you. It's up to you if you stay or go – it might be good to be away, take the time to clear your head and get ready for your whole life to turn upside down? Most men get a pregnancy to watch to prepare themselves for that. You've had a couple of days at best. This is going fast, Jake,'

'Do you not want me?'

'JAKE! Shut up. I am pretty much sitting on my hands to stop myself from flinging myself at you. All I want is you.'

'Then isn't that enough?' he asked.

'I'm just worried–' Silva replied

'Stop just worrying.' he said, sweeping her up in his arms and kissing her, really kissing her, and she didn't stop him this time, instead, something in his kiss told her that nothing else was more important than this and she – and her body - agreed.

Her body was his the second he pulled her top off, his as she fumbled with his jeans, and he was hers as he tugged at her skinny jeans with frustration. They held their breath tight as the baby monitor scuffled but then went quiet again. This time, he remembered to use a condom.

This time, they would remember the experience.

'Bed. Not sofa.' Silva murmured into Jake's ear and somehow, they crept to her room, though her heart was loud in her ears, and she couldn't see how Rose hadn't woken from the drumming of it. They made it to the bed, and in the early-dwindling winter light, found each other at last in urgent motion and breaths.

'I want to take you out on dates,' Jake said, fingers interlinked with hers as they lay sweaty and happily in bed.

'We've done everything backwards, haven't we? Had a baby, this, and *now* you want to date me?! I feel like you should move in first, and then we can go on our first date.'

Jake laughed, 'don't tell my mum that. She'll be gutted to lose me.'

'Bless. Rose is going to wake up for food soon. At least, she had better, or she won't sleep tonight.'

'We can get up in a minute. You can teach me what cuisine

means to a baby.'

'Okay. And maybe while you feed her and have her decorate you, I can shower.' Silva said although she didn't want to lose the scent of his nice aftershave from her neck, her hair...but it would stay in her bed if she was a little bit gross and didn't change it, she supposed.

'Nothing like the deep end!'

'Nope.'

Rose fussed on the monitor and Silva automatically got up out of bed.

'You didn't even think about that.'

Silva shrugged and quickly threw a jumper and some old pyjama bottoms on.

'I'm trained to auto-respond to Madam Rose, good sir. Now get up and help me,' she grinned and left to pick up Rose who was chewing on her blanket.

Jake ran into the living room to put his clothes back on and listened to Silva talking to their baby. *"Their". Weird.*

'Hey, little one. Do you want some food? You have the grand choice of some veggies and rice or... veggies and a chicken? What will it be for you today? And do you want a bath? Do you want to put Daddy through the joys of washing the hair of a baby who hates that? Ah, he is listening – we cannot give away *all* our secrets. Be a good girl and brew a nappy for him, won't you?' Silva was smiling to herself as she said it. It was both nice and weird to refer to Jake as "Daddy".

'So mean.' Jake said, re-clothed and having put the kettle on. Silva passed Rose to him and he bounced her around.

Silva showed him what Rose was having for dinner; steamed carrots and broccoli with some plain chicken. She let Jake feed Rose, who was surprisingly receptive, only coating a little bit of him with it when she sneezed.

'I think I'm okay at this!'

'Yep. You have a knack. But do watch her. She likes to hide handfuls of it and paint herself. I'm going to make a cup of tea, do you want one? Then off to see mummy?'

'Can I come back after?'

'Of course, but only if your mum is all right.'

'I could tell her tomorrow...'

'Oh, you are so persuasive. At least tell her you aren't coming home tonight...'

Jake grinned and Silva kissed him. Rose took the opportunity to smear carrot into her hair, face, and as they would soon discover, ears.

She clapped, thrilled with herself.

'I should probably be disgusted by that, but I feel very warm and fuzzy.'

'If you liked that, you'll LOVE nappies.' Silva laughed. Together they limited some of the damage and cleaned her up.

'Silv, have you farted?' Jake asked as they finally all sat down, Rose on the floor with her toys, and the adults had a lukewarm cup of tea each.

Silva looked offended and then grinned.

'Welcome to nappy and bath time.'

An hour later, Rose was changed, clean, and in fresh sleep-wear and once again playing, this time with a lamp on rather than the light. Silva had removed the noisy toys.

'You're getting her ready to sleep again...clever.'

'She won't for another hour or so but it helps her to learn evenings. I then of course spoil it by letting her watch TV with me.'

'How do you *remember* all this stuff every day? How do you still manage to get dressed? How are you still going?'

'I'm taking all of this as a compliment to my multitasking skills. And here is the point where most adults think "I haven't had dinner yet. I should fix that." but I'm normally too exhausted. And then it's toast o'clock if I'm that hungry.'

'I'm going to see what you've got in your fridge and make something. You must have *something* edible.'

Jake disappeared and returned minutes later, having turned the oven on to grill omelettes.

'This is why we need you. To avoid scurvy from only eating bread.'

'Rose won't get it. You will.' Jake grunted. 'I called my mum, I'm going to take her out for brunch tomorrow and I'll tell her then. And maybe you can come over after for a cuppa with Rose if she wants that?'

'Sounds like a plan.'

'I meant what I said, you know.' Jake said, as he served their omelettes and put aside a little bowl for Rose to try when it was cooler. She was already sniffing the air. Silva wondered if her innate love of food came from her or Jake or if babies were just… always hungry.

'About what?'

'I want to take you out on dates. Do this properly. Go for dinner somewhere nice. Cinema.'

'An actual sit-down dinner with no surprise poo or sick or my food going cold or getting stolen? And no washing up? Wearing clothes without sick on them. Maybe even makeup. Sounds like actual heaven to me,' Silva said. 'Count me in.'

Rose shuffled her way to the sofa – not quite crawling, but trying - and sat up, then held her arms out upward with pleading eyes.

'She's like a dog!' Jake said, laughing.

'Yes. Only stinkier, and not house trained. Pick her up, she can watch a film with us? Nothing gory. She likes 80's and 90's cartoons and films, but anything colourful is fine – Layla shows her drag queens all day…'

'How about Treasure Planet? Not seen that for ages and it's on catch up from Christmas.'

'Perfect.'

'Silv. Look.' Jake whispered a little while later. Silva, engrossed in the film, looked over. Rose had wriggled over to Jake and was asleep on him, his arm around her.

'That cannot be comfortable against your skinny ribs.' Silva whispered back, but she was smiling and her eyes were filling.

'I'll have you know I'm a champion pillow.' Jake replied. He tried to shift gently to give Rose a nicer pose but gave up and

Silva put a blanket on her.

The film ended and Rose showed no sign of moving.

'How long do you have left here now, Jake?'

'I fly out on the fifth. In the evening,' he checked his watch. 'Now would be a good time to call the office, if anyone is in.'

Silva nodded, 'best cram in a date or two first, then.'

Jake smiled. 'We can arrange that. For now. Shall we get her to bed, and I'll try to call work?'

Silva lifted Rose carefully and carried her to her bed, where she stirred at the cool mattress compared to Jake's warmth but settled. Jake couldn't get through to the office, so he and Silva went to bed, too, but didn't sleep for a long time. It was just as well Layla was not home.

*

The next day, Silva fixed her mascara and fussed in the mirror. She bent into the pram and picked lint off Rose's clothes. Her phone buzzed. Jake. *Come now.* Silva took a deep breath, left the cubicle, and walked with shaky legs to meet her new mother-in-law. Rose's grandmother.

She wheeled the pram into the café around the corner and took a deep breath.

Jake waved back, and Olivia looked white as a sheet but otherwise – bar a few grey hairs – exactly as Silva remembered her.

Silva rolled in, parked the pram facing outwards and sat next to her daughter with a breath held in her chest.

'Would you like a drink?' a waitress asked.

'A hot chocolate, please,' Silva said, clocking the full mugs of Jake and Olivia. Rose could share hers but the chances were that she would be napping shortly.

'So, Silva.' Olivia began and looked at Silva levelly.

'It's lovely to see you.' Silva said truthfully and Jake nudged his knee against hers. 'I'm sorry about the shock.'

'You too, dear. I'm just in a state of surprise – I always wanted Jake to have his own family – but not quite like this – I'm sure you understand – I can't believe how silly you both were.'

'I know. We are too old to have acted like that.'

'You are. But. Just look at her. She's lovely.' Olivia said, her whole face softening.

'She is. I really want you to bond with her. Spend time with her. If you would like that.'

'Of course I would. And anytime you need a break, or someone to take care of her, you bring her to me.'

Silva let go of her tense breath and smiled.

'Thank you.'

'My pleasure, dear. How have you been on your own? Will you be okay when Jake goes back to America?'

'I think so. I have my own business, so it's tricky sometimes. I have an amazing friend who helps me out, and a childminder now and then. Really, it's fine. How have you been? I feel like it's been a long time since I saw you and you made us breakfast sandwiches for our hangovers.' Silva said as Rose started to protest about being stuck in her pram while she could sense someone close by who liked babies. She unclipped her and picked her up.

'I've been good, yeah. Got a little dog.'

'He's massive.' Jake cut in.

'Okay, I got a medium dog. Been on a few cruises. Oh, Jake tells me you decorate – I'd love for you to come and give me a few ideas.'

'Sure, I'd love to! Do you want to – hold her? She seems interested in you.' Silva said, offering Rose up like a sacrifice.

Olivia took the proffered infant and Silva thanked the waitress, taking her hot chocolate from her. Olivia's eyes shone and she smiled and sat Rose down on her lap, bouncing her. Rose grabbed one of her fingers and started babbling at her. Silva raised her eyebrows at Jake and they both smiled.

'I'm going to the loo.' he said.

Olivia leaned in when he was out of earshot.

'I know this wasn't planned,' she said, while Rose took her opportunity to take a handful of cream from her mother's drink and shove it in her mouth before she could be stopped, 'but would you have picked him? Had this not happened? I know you had a thing when you were younger.'

'Olivia...'

'Liv is fine.'

'Liv, to be honest, your son is generous and sweet, but I didn't have him pegged as interested in a life like this, especially not with me... and I didn't have it pegged for me either. But I'm glad it's him. It is certainly complicated. But I'm happy.'

'Good.' Liv exhaled. 'You have an interesting story to tell Rose one day!' she said. Silva sipped her hot chocolate and put it back out of reach of Rose, who was already covered in whipped cream.

'Don't we just.' Silva said as Jake returned from the cash register.

'I'm having an idea, Mum. I think we should all go shopping – Silv desperately needs some new clothes.'

'Rude.' Silva said, although she knew he was right.

'I'm not saying you're not gorgeous, I'm not saying you're shabby, but that top has more holes in it than the moon does craters and your wardrobe looks like it was invaded by a herd of moths. Please. I have money I can't spend because all I do is work. Can I please treat the three women in my life to some shopping?'

'Oh, go on then, Jake. You drive a hard bargain here.' Liv said and smiled. 'Silva, for once – let yourself be taken care of. I know it's hard as a mum, but it's just some clothes and stuff, okay? He might even let you buy dinner later,' she said and winked.

'Not a chance.' Silva heard Jake mutter.

They set off for the shopping centre, Jake pushing the pram while Liv held Rose and showed her the various sights of the town. Silva felt odd, her hands free, but liked it.

After a heavy day of shopping, in which Silva had gotten carried away, they collapsed on Liv's sofas with cups of tea and a takeaway.

'Success, don't you think?' Jake said, looking relieved.

'Absolutely. Thanks for the clothes.'

'Just providing for my family.' He winked. Silva's stomach

fluttered with an awkward mix of gratitude, love, and a tug of embarrassment that she felt like she was losing her self-sufficiency.

'Hi, Mum. Are you all right to talk?' Silva asked as the mobile connected her later. Silva was in new pyjamas that were not full of holes, new slippers and although she still felt awkward about it – she also felt very blessed.
Jake had pretty much bought Rose everything Disney, and Silva wasn't going to complain. She thumbed Rose's new Minnie Mouse playsuit.

'Absolutely.' she replied. 'Everything okay?'

'Yeah. You know how I said the father wasn't interested in Rose…'

'Yeah…'

'Well, the truth is I didn't know who it was. But Rose's eyes are green all of a sudden. Jake's green. She's his. We're – making a go of it.'

'You don't have to trick him! It will come back on you.'

'Wow, Mum, just…wow. Do you think I put contact lenses on a baby?! I'll send you a photo of the two of them together… and some of him as a baby. You can see the clone I birthed!'

'Okay,' she said, laughing. 'I'm glad he wants to be involved. That's good.'
Silva smiled into the phone and listened to her mother talk about Spain, their renovations, and life. She wondered what her dad would think of this. She thought that he would probably laugh then slap Jake round the side of the head, and then tell Silva she was getting chubby.
Eventually, her mother ran out of things to ramble about, and they said their goodbyes.

'So that's them all told, then.' Jake said as Silva sat on the sofa. Rose looked at her quizzically then threw herself at Silva. 'Bar my boss. He emailed to say he will call me back.'
Silva nodded and gave him a sad smile.

'She doesn't want to see me when you're here.' Jake pouted.

'She is just more used to me. You will have lots of time to spend together. I can go be somewhere else if you want.'

'No – I didn't mean for you to go, I just mean…'

'She's a baby. She isn't favouring me to get at you.' Silva grinned. 'Babies are not vindictive at all.'

'I know that. I mean. My rational brain knows that.'

'You've bought her a lot of stuff today. I know in your head that's cemented this for you – and it's really nice to touch something and think, "Rose, your father bought you that" but she is still seven months old. She doesn't understand money, or clothes, or anything. Just being clean, warm and fed, entertained, and loved. She needs time with you.'

'Which I'm running out of.'

'Do you have any clients tomorrow?'

'One. A dinner one. Then the day after… evening flight. Unless Boss says otherwise.'

'How about…I go into the office tomorrow daytime. Do some work. I have some designs to draw up with Eric ready for installs next week, and our foot traffic before Christmas increased, so he thinks we should be in anyway. You could go for a walk. Spend time together. I'll be on the end of the phone if you need me.'

'That sounds like a great idea,' he said. 'What am I going to tell my boss when he asks how my Christmas was?'

'Err, the truth?'

'Oh yes sure, "hi boss, just before I started this job I had a leaving party, and at that party, I got someone pregnant. Could I have belated paternity leave? Yes, she is seven months old."'

'Paternity leave isn't a terrible idea, in all fairness.' Silva said. 'Give us a chance to… work this out. It's amazing, but it's all still very new. Early doors. I want *you.* I want that date. This all feels like a rush.'

'I know. I know. But what do I say?'

'You say: "something has come up with my family" and if they ask more then you explain that you recently found out you had a little girl and you need some time to process that and get to know her. How do you think it's been for me? I was pregnant and then had a baby for 7 months and trying to explain my situation was awkward each time, and the pity from people…but you won't get that.' Silva said bitterly. 'They will probably congratulate you as if that's normal!'

'Don't snap. I know – you did all that by yourself, which is amazing, but you did it all by choice…this is all new to me, and I'm not as brave as you!'

A dangerous edge flicked Silva's tone as she said, 'you are choosing this, aren't you? If you aren't, you need to leave. Don't confuse her to not bother again. She deserves more than that.'

'That isn't what I said, Silv. I just mean – it's complicated,' he said, rubbing her knee. Rose started to cry at their raised voices.

'Sssh, Rose, it's okay.' Silva said and lifted her pyjama top. Rose latched with a bit of tooth. Silva winced and took another deep breath.

'Nothing is being sorted right now. Take tomorrow with her. Think about what your plan is for your boss. Talk to him, please. I obviously don't want you to go back so soon – at all. But you had that commitment long before…and May is only a few months away. We can do this.'

Jake sighed. 'Thank you.'

'You good? Got nappies…snacks…clothes?' Silva checked the next morning.

'Yes, yes, yes.' Jake said, heaving the bag onto Rose's pram and trying not to wince.

'Have fun. Call me if you need *anything*.' Silva said as she left the flat in good time and in new clothes. She kissed Jake goodbye, then Rose, who clapped her hands happily.

*

'Silva! You're early!' Eric said cheerfully.

'Yes. And baby-free. And I have breakfast.'

'Wow. And – new clothes I spy? Stain and hole-free jeans? Wow. What happened to YOU?' Eric said. 'Oh – and the glow. Oh,

I get it, she has a new MAN!'

Silva blushed, grateful no clients were in yet.

'Calm down, I'll tell you over coffee. I think we can spare ten minutes of a working day, especially as there is no small one to occupy.'

'I actually like having Rose here. The clients love her, she makes a good screen break.'

'She's not a puppy!'

'Well, to me, she is.'

Silva rolled her eyes and filled Eric in. His hands never left his face – covering his mouth in shock, wiping tears from his eyes or just leaning on his hand in riveted curiosity.

'Wow. And to think, all I did on New Year's was gain half a stone on Twiglets and sherry and annoy my aunt by beating her at monopoly. Oh, and I finally perfected poached eggs.'

'Sounds delightfully boring. I think I need a break to get over that break!'

'If you need time, I'm sure I can deal…'

'No really. It's all right. Just intense. Like last night – went from a bickering argument to amazing sex in about ten minutes.'

'Ah, I miss true love. Silv, remember you haven't had a boyfriend in ages. That's pretty normal – the only difference is 1) you've known him for years so already know how to irritate each other and 2) you have a baby together, and while it's not new for you to have a baby, it's new knowledge that she is his too and it is ALL new for him.'

'You talk sense.' Silva said, booting up her laptop and finishing off her pastry. 'Thanks.'

Silva's day passed quickly, all emails answered, several unscheduled consultations given and some more work booked in, and she and Eric managed to finalise some designs over lunch baguettes from Layla's café.

She checked her phone regularly, expecting panicked messages from Jake or at least for him to ask for advice, but had nothing, just a few photos of them playing at the park and of Rose having her nap.

When she arrived home later, it was to an eerily empty flat. Eerier still, it was tidier than she had left it. Confused, she made herself a coffee, changed into pyjamas and ate a bowl of cereal she didn't have to share. As lovely as it was, it felt odd.

The door clicked open a little while later and she jumped up to help as Jake pushed the pram into the hallway.

'Hey. How was work?' he asked.

'Good, how was...parenting?' Silva asked.

'Exhausting. But great.' he replied, his eyes shining happily. 'We shared an ice cream and that is a disaster right now, so please judge me not on the most recent but the rest of the day.'

'Ha! You are brave to tackle ice cream on your first solo day out! It's cool, there's no test. I'll put her in the bath after you've had a shower.'

'Ah yes, work. Silv, how do you have energy for work as well?'

'You don't. You have caffeine, hope, and the knowledge that work means talking to an adult for a bit so you crack on with it. You'll be fine.'

Jake watched for a moment as Silva released her sticky baby from the pram and grinned at her.

'You look so pleased with yourself. Look at your crusty ice-cream quiff! Have you had a nice day with Daddy? Has he filled you with sugar for me to deal with? Oh yes, he has. Good lad. Exactly what I would have done to him. Ok.' Silva hauled a laughing Rose up. 'Time to get you fed and washed. And then some energy burned off.'

Jake grinned at them and slipped off to the bathroom, where the noisy old shower did little to drown out his racing thoughts.

Jake emerged from the bedroom clean, in his trademark black jeans, a blazer and polished shoes as Silva was finishing feeding Rose.

'You look sexy.' Silva told him as Rose painted her hair green with chewed-up peas.

'Thanks. Right. I will see you tonight. I'll try to bring you a doggy bag.'

Jake returned later with salted caramel cheesecake and was rewarded well. He also returned with bad news, but he didn't know how to say it, so he kept it inside.

Jake woke up before Silva did and lay, watching her sleep. Wondering how long before Rose he had woken, if he felt confident enough to be the first face she saw this morning or if she would cry so hard she woke Silva. This was all so strange and new, but wonderful, too. And today it all had to end for a few months.

'We never got our date.' Silva said in a sad sleepy voice.

'I know. But we will soon. When I come back. Soon.'

Silva sighed sadly and stretched. 'I'm not going to work today.'

Jake smiled into her hair and kissed her head.

'Good.' he said as Silva fell back to sleep.

Jake eventually needed a pee and untangled himself from Silva, accidentally woke Rose up by flushing the toilet, her confused whimper betraying her as awake.

'Good morning Rose.' Jake said, picking her up. She was looking at him with curious eyes, not crying, just calm. He smiled. She returned it. He changed her nappy, which she kicked off about, then wrestled her into a new outfit.

Silva still wasn't awake.

Now what? Jake wondered as he carried Rose into the living room and turned the TV on quietly. He put a movie on for her, just one picked at random, and she seemed happy enough. He poured himself a bowl of cereal and thought about what he needed to do; packing was sorted. Everything crammed into a hand luggage case, ready to collect from his mum's later. As if there was so little for him to take from here to there. As if he didn't suddenly have a daughter, a girlfriend, a life and reasons to stay.

Rose put her hand in his cereal and made mush of his Cheerios.

Oh. You have to feed the baby, too. He thought and smiled, navigated her into her high chair and made her some porridge with jam and mashed banana in it, eating his Cheerios out of her reach.

'It looks like she's eating blood.' Silva said, laughing as she came into the living room.

'Yep. I do have regrets about not putting her in clothes *before* breakfast.'

Silva laughed. 'She would have found a way to get covered in *something* before ten a.m. You're doing good.' Silva kissed him, then planted a kiss on the back of Rose's head, where there was no second-hand food to accidentally eat.

'What's your plan today?'

'Leave for the airport at 8. Other than that, spend time with you. Early dinner with Mum – would you like to come? I'm cooking so there will be loads.'

'It has all come round so fast. Jesus. You're going to leave for four months. She'll almost be a year old.'

'I know, Silv, I know.'

'Did your boss ever call you?'

'He did last night. I told him. He said he can't spare me, but he'll try to as soon as he can.'

Silva sighed sadly. 'Okay. Let's just enjoy today, shall we?' she said, her eyes sad and her face pale. Jake nodded and together they cleaned Rose up.

The day went too quickly; they spent it at the zoo, taking hundreds of photos, each tinged with a little bit of sadness that Silva tried to quash.

I could call the airport and report a bomb threat. She thought in her wilder plans to keep Jake there. *No, too many repercussions.* Instead, she watched Jake showing Rose the lions – or was he showing the lions Rose? The lioness licked her lips hungrily at the podgy, delicious baby just a few inches away. Rose laughed, unaware that she could be dinner.

Later, at dinner, Rose ate a surprising portion for a seven-month-old whereas Silva could barely eat. The mood was light enough; they told Liv about the zoo, their sped-up new family life, Rose's funny ways. Liv agreed to take Rose a few times a week for Silva to go out and do manual decorating again and enjoy herself. Jake felt the sadness of life and plans building around him but squashed it down.

Too soon, it was time to say goodbye. They all hugged Liv goodbye and went back to Silva's for the last hour of Jake's time. Rose slept off her impressive dinner and Jake and Silva looked at each other, tears forming.

They lay in bed together. Physical goodbyes over, Silva finally let some tears out.

'Please try your boss again.' she asked.

Jake's heart plummeted. 'You know it won't change his answer.'

Silva shook her head, sudden frustrated rage filling her.

'No, I don't know that, Jake. If it was my employee I'd tell them not to get the plane. I'd tell them to cradle their new kid close, not to worry about work. This is the problem with big soulless companies...'

'This has just happened at a bad time...' Jake tried to reason with her.

'OH I'M SO SORRY JAKE. I'LL RESCHEDULE, SHALL I? Pause your daughter where she is so you can go off and work in a different country? Maybe we are better off alone if you don't care. Go on.' Silva tore out of bed and pulled her pyjamas on. 'I opened my life to you, Jake. I opened my heart. and Rose's, too, and this is what you do? You don't even fucking TRY to have more time with us?'

'I'm sorry.' Jake said. 'I honestly think I'll be fine to come back in a few weeks.'

'That's great then. I'll see you then I guess. Go say goodbye to Rose.'

'Are you serious?'

'Fucking deadly, Jake. Go.' Silva snapped, feeling rage pour through her blood and the racing of it making her heart slam against her chest.

Jake's eyes stung with tears but he stood up, hurriedly put some clothes on and took a moment to himself as Silva stormed out of the bedroom. *I've ruined everything.* He thought to himself.

He kissed a sleeping Rose on her forehead and whispered a good-bye to her, then went to the living room to Silva.

'Forgive me for not being instantly perfect at this. Were you, Silv? Five, six days ago I had no responsibilities and no plans past May. I don't know how to be some perfect dad who doesn't leave, but I have commitments... I think I need time, too. I didn't think I did but...'

Silva was worryingly calm in her response, 'Rose comes first, Jake. She needs stability. You can have as much space as you want but don't you dare come back if you aren't intending to stay in her life.'

'I'll be back as soon as I can.' He said and made for the door.

'Don't trouble yourself too much.' Silva said, raw spite in her voice.

He had never heard her speak to anyone like that before. He didn't know what else to do; he whispered, 'I love you.' and left, taking care to close the door gently.

After she had calmed down, Silva couldn't believe the door had clicked. That things had ended quite like this. Silence pierced her flat in a way she had never felt before, and she cried until her eyes were raw.

CHAPTER 14

'My throat hurts.' Silva lied to Layla when she asked why she and Rose were sat eating ice lollies in January. Layla nodded at her, got one too, and sat on the sofa with Silva.

'Jake told me what happened.' Layla said, looking at Silva's puffy eyes. 'Are you okay?'

'Have you taken sides yet?' Silva asked her voice hoarse from crying.

'I'm a grown adult woman, Silv. I'm not doing sides unless one of you cheats on the other.' Layla said, rolling their eyes. 'Just tell me if you're okay or not.'

'Yes. I am. I have to be, don't I? What option do I have? Get over it or pine forever over him – when he obviously doesn't care?'

'Silv... you know that he does. He is just bad at this. A bit thoughtless sometimes. Good intentions but bad follow-through. You've seen it so many times with his exes. You've used it as a "thank goodness I'm not with him" before.'

'True.'

'So why do you think he will be magically different for you?'

Silva just stared at Layla in response.

'Exactly. And have you been perfect, my love? You are no-toriously hard to get close to. You've done well – so little time with him and you opened up this much – but were you always perfectly reasonable? Rational? Ready to accept things may be harder?'

Silva fussed over Rose's hair to avoid Layla's eye. Layla laughed.

'I thought not.'

'Lay, how do you find it so easy?'

'HA! I do not. I have trust issues. Fleeing your own family will do that to you. I constantly think Opal is a hidden camera girlfriend. It's hard to be her boss and her partner. I wonder what she's doing with me. If she is going back to being straight and I'm just a divorce madness. But...you can't live with all of that. Sure, you have to feel your feelings. Try and let them out, but you'll go mad if you always listen to that sour inner voice. She could choose anyone else if she wanted. I can't do much about that. I just want to enjoy what we have and work on it.'

'You're very wise. I've missed you.' Silva said. 'How are things with Opal?'

'Good actually. We are looking for a place together. We have our eye on one and just waiting...'

'Oh, wow. That's brilliant. You're leaving me?!'

'Yes, Silv, it's time. You have Jake to help you. I need to move on but yes – still available to help you look after her. I would miss her too much otherwise.'

Silva grinned. 'She is pretty hard to live without.'

'Silv, you know that this isn't going to be a "he comes along and everything is ok" type deal. Like you won't be happy ever after because a guy turned up to save you? Nope. Life isn't like that. You have done loads of work on yourself and your business and you should be proud. Falling in love is a bonus as well as finding Rose's dad and all that. Great news for both of you, but you are human individuals adapting to a big shock and he has a bit more shock to adapt to, and if you think it's all running off into the sunset now, you're kidding yourselves. You need time to yourselves and space for each other. Go out. When he's back. Date. We can babysit. You are still people. You need to do things and work things out and live.'

'I think it's too late.'

'You know it isn't.' Layla squeezed her hand. 'Now. Let's get up. Go out and do something, shall we?'

*

Silva heard nothing from Jake for a couple of weeks. Layla was slowly but surely moving out; all their clothes were gone. Their bedding and furniture remained. Despite having Rose with her, the flat was too quiet, and Silva felt too sad to spend much time there. Rose went to Liv's a few times while Silva went to work, enjoying getting her frustration out on old, bad wallpaper and ripping rooms apart to rebuild them.

She returned home one afternoon to have a shower before collecting Rose – she was caked in paint - to find Jake at her doorstep. She dropped her keys on the floor and felt her cheeks rush red. She was rooted to the spot, resisting the urge to get closer to him. To push him or kiss him. She waited. Her stomach flipped.

'I've moved back to England.' Jake said. His beautiful green eyes were dark and shiny.

Silva kept waiting.

'I'm sorry. I truly am. Can we try again, please?'

'I thought things were critical in America.'

Jake flushed with embarrassment.

'I was so stupid to put that before you. I spent a week or so out there before I realised how stupid it was that I was out there and my life is *here*. I tied things up – apologised to my boss – and came back as soon as I could.'

'Did he let you keep your job here?'

'For now, yes. I don't think he was amused.'

'Okay.'

'What is?'

'Jake… I never wanted you to jeopardise your job for this. What hurt was that you didn't even ask properly for an extension. I shouldn't have flipped though, I'm sorry, I took out my fear on you. It was like we didn't matter to you enough to try.'

'I know. I'm sorry. I was too scared…I was still a bit in shock. I couldn't work out what to say to ask.' He said, looking depleted. Silva let his words hang for a moment.

'But this,' Silva said, relenting, unable to stop a grin leaking out. 'This makes it better,' she said, grabbing him and coating him in flecks of dried paint and plaster.

'You smell like a hardware store.'

'Sexy, right. The reunion that you pictured. I'll go shower.'

'Don't bother.' Jake winked. 'I like this look on you.'

Silva snorted and picked up her keys to let them in.

'I have conditions,' Silva said, probably too late, as they had already ripped their clothes off, snowing paint and plaster dust and they were so close together and kissing, and she wasn't sure her front door was quite closed but she didn't care just then.

'I want a real date. Real *dates*. I want you to move in properly after we have some. I want to do this right, Jake. And I'm going to get you doing the washing up.'

'Deal. I'll take you out tonight, and I promise to do some washing up sometimes.'

'You cook a lot so of course, it's fine to share it...but I don't think I've ever seen you so much as touch a sponge? How did you cope in America?'

Jake blushed and confessed, 'my apartment had an option to add on someone to do the cleaning and take care of my laundry too, so I basically just lived like I was at Mum's...but in America... and without my mum.'

Silva laughed, 'I thought it seemed like you'd adapted fast. Now I know your secret...I can't believe you paid someone to do your washing! Don't you worry, I'll get you cleaning.'

Jake smiled. 'I can't wait. You have to be patient with me and let me learn though, I know what you're like. You'll get fed up with me getting it wrong.'

'Well, you'll just have to listen to me properly the first time then.' Silva said. 'So. You're taking me out then? Is that so there's no washing up?'

'Ha! No, you just deserve to get taken out for a nice meal.'

Silva's stomach did a flip. 'What about Rose?'

'Mum has our backs there. She has sleep stuff for her, doesn't she?'

'Yup.' Silva said and let their bodies take over, amazed that just a little while ago she was still heavy-hearted and sad and lonely and now...she was back in his arms, their bodies connecting. It was amazing how fast things could and did change.

Jake nudged Silva awake a little bit later.

'Hey, you. We have a dinner reservation in an hour and a half. Get ready. I'm going to go to Mum's and get something to wear and a takeaway for her. Okay?'

Silva stretched and grinned, 'yes, boss. Tough life for me. See you soon.'

An hour and a half later, Silva was scrubbed clean and in a new dress that she had bought for herself. It had been expensive, but beautiful, and she had had nowhere to wear it, until now.

'Where did you get THAT?' Jake exclaimed as he opened the taxi door for her.

Silva laughed, 'just a present to myself.'

Jake smiled in response and wolf-whistled.

They ate Italian food in a restaurant with a ceiling painted to look like stars.

'The food is *beautiful.*' Silva said, though she was regretting ordering tagliatelle, having forgotten the level of organisation it would take to eat without making a mess or embarrassing herself. Somehow, she pulled it off but while everything looked, felt and tasted beautiful, something felt odd.

'Isn't it? I thought you would like how they decorate... and I like the food. I thought it was a nice mix of both of us.'

'It is,' Silva said happily, hoping Jake would tell her if she had food on her face. 'It's a great choice.'

'Thank you. Would you like dessert?'

'Can't hurt to look.' Silva winked.

'I'm not ready for this evening to be over yet,' Silva said a little later, swaying a bit after polishing off the last of their wine and a complimentary limoncello.

'What do you want to do?'

'Relive some past. Drink the cheapest wine we can and sit on the canal.'

Jake laughed and steered her to an off licence.

'WAIT! You have to get a stranger to buy it for us.' Silva insisted. Jake cajoled a homeless stranger into accepting twenty pounds for cheap wine on the proviso he could keep the change.

They ran to the canal laughing with their wine, ignoring the signs warning them not to drink in the area and passed the bottle to each other.

'It tastes like sour fruit and burning lungs.' Jake said with a grimace.

'It's supposed to,' Silva laughed but could feel her throat protesting and burning in her chest. 'How on earth did we stand this?'

'No idea,' Jake said and hauled himself up. Silva stayed where she was, legs swinging. 'I'll come back.'
Jake returned a few minutes later, with a bottle of red wine.

'This will be better. Some things can change in our memories.'
Silva took a swig from the bottle.

'Oh my word, that tastes like...warmth. Fireplaces. I sound like a wanker. I thought red wine was just vinegar. Or something you put in a stew...'

'Welcome to the good bits of being a grown-up, my love.'
A moment passed, the sound of water moving and people talking nearby adding a backing track.

'I'm sorry I kicked off so hard before, when you had to go back to America. I find it hard to need you, and I dealt with it badly, and spent every moment you were gone regretting it.'

Jake wrapped his arm around her and sighed. 'You already apologised for that. I didn't do very well either. How about...we just try to grow together. You tell me when you're scared and want to take Rose and run for the hills, live in your hut independently and eat grizzly bears, and I'll remind you that I'm not that scary. And I'll tell you when I need you to give me some of your brave.'

Silva laughed. 'I don't have much brave.'

'Of course you do. So much. You're raising a baby, building a business and now starting a relationship with me even though your instincts push me away from you. *So much brave.*'
She rested her head on his shoulder to hide the hot tears coming at how much of her he could just *see.*

'Thank you. There's no like…guidance for this, not sure an agony aunt has ever come across this before. And if we don't want this anymore… Rose is the priority.'

'Yes, Silv. Now drink this wine, enjoy this night. I love you.' They took a couple of hours to finish that bottle and a second one and somehow avoided detection from patrolling police officers as they watched the streetlamps reflecting on the water, which rippled as the wind picked up.

'What is it you really want out of life, Jake?' Silva asked, her head on his shoulder.

'I don't know.' Jake said. 'I was always so intent on getting a good job that I didn't think about it. But I guess it would be something to do with food. A restaurant or something.'

'That's nothing like what you do now. Why aren't you doing that?!'

'It feels too late to start.'

'Jake, you're only 28.'

'I know. But for now, I think I'm good for change for a bit.' he said, tickling her ribs.

She laughed. 'Okay, I'll back off.'

'What do *you* want out of life?' he asked her.

'I think I already have it. I like my job and business. I have you. I have Rose. I'm happy. Of course, I would love my dad back. Or to have been a rock star. But I'm okay with not being what 15-year-old me wanted. I'm what 29-year-old me wants.'

'There's still time to be a rock star.'

'I'm in bed by ten most nights. I'm not sure I have the energy. Maybe in an alternate universe I rock the stage and love it, but here and now is just fine by me.' Silva enjoyed the cold around her feet as she spoke. Jake smiled at her.

'Okay. Fair enough. Can we get up now? I think I'm going to get frostbite soon if we don't.'

'I suppose so.' Silva replied and wiggled backwards before scrabbling to get up in an undignified manner. 'Wow, that is harder than you would think when everything has gone numb.'

'And you're fairly pissed, wearing silly heels and a dress.'

'Be quiet and take me to bed.'

'Gladly.'

*

'I feel like all I do is mess things up and get told off by you.' Jake said, one afternoon a few weeks later.

'I don't mean to tell you off. I'm just trying to show you.' Silva said as she showed him her tricks to keep Rose entertained, fed and bathed all in the space of an hour. To Jake, an hour had never gone so simultaneously quickly or slowly.

'I'll never be good at this.' he said. He had bath bubbles in his ear.

'You think I am?! I've messed up so many times. I've had crying and screaming competitions with her. I have almost dropped her. I've almost forgotten her in the middle of a shop because I got distracted and I feel like I'm failing most days. I'm usually so exhausted I could weep. Darling. You're doing fine. As long as the right person is pooping their pants, I think we'll be okay. Just having you here – feeling like I'm not taking the piss always dropping her on Layla – that's such a relief. And having your mum, too.' Silva said, gently removing Rose's fingers from the plug without breaking eye contact with him. Rose grumbled but then happily splashed them both as revenge for having her plans scuppered.

'See? How did you know she was going to do that?'

'Because she is a nine-month-old baby who has just dis-covered the nature of the speed she can move at. And she went quiet. A dead giveaway that she's up to something. We have plenty of time. And she adores you. You're doing fine. That's one of the few things we need not worry about.' Silva replied.
Jake smiled in relief. Silva smiled back and handed him Rose's towel so he could pull her out of the bath. They got her to sleep after an hour of negotiating, coddling, and frustration.

'She never used to fight sleep this much,' Silva said. 'Must be the effects of getting older. We must be more exciting than we gave ourselves credit for.'

'Maybe.' Jake said. 'Wine?' he asked hopefully after they

were certain Rose was asleep.

Silva bit her lip. 'I'm not sure I can, Jake.'

'Why not?'

'I'm late for my period.' she said and watched his face go through a kaleidoscope of different colours.

CHAPTER 15

'Say something, Jake.' Silva pleaded. 'I would *love* a glass of wine but I...'

'Can we get a test before we get our hopes up?' Jake said simply. Silva smiled, her heart pounding.

'Yes but...we don't know how accurate it will be or how far along I am. When I was six weeks with Rose, I started feeling rotten, had awful sickness...nothing like that yet. I'll go get a couple of tests.'

Silva poured him a wine, kissed him, and left the flat as quietly as she could.

Silva browsed the pharmacy, plucking up the nerve to go to the pregnancy tests, feeling a weird tingle in her stomach. *I like not knowing just for a little while,* she thought.

'Silva?' said a familiar voice behind her. Silva turned.

'Layla! Hey! Are you okay?'

'Yeah, fine. Just toothache and trying to avoid the dentist. You?'

'Just some Calpol for Rose. We're running out; she has a bit of a cold.' Silva said. She felt awful lying, especially after all Layla had done for her, but she was excited to have this as just for Jake and her for those first few days, if not weeks.

'Oh bless her! Let me know if you need anything... miss you.'

'Miss you too.' Silva said, cheeks flushed at of course bumping into Layla now, of all times. Silva hugged Layla, who paid and left, then quickly bought the tests and hurried home before she bumped into anyone else.

*

'It's positive.' Jake said after Silva couldn't look. He beamed at her. 'This is amazing news.'

Silva smiled back. 'We just got into a routine...is it okay to admit I'm scared? I'll have two kids under two...

'*We* will have two under two. It will be all right.' Jake said. Silva squeezed his hand and went to tinker with her guitar to clear her mind of swimming thoughts.

'You're good, you could be famous.' Jake said after she put the guitar down and Rose clapped determinedly, making her parents laugh.

*

The weeks skipped by fast. Liv was thrilled by the news. Even Joyce seemed to be happy for them, sending a bunch of flowers and a bottle of champagne. Silva had grinned at the impracticality of that gift, but, as Jake pointed out, it meant she was trying. Silva felt stronger and happier as time passed, her days passing fast, work busy, and Rose was trying to start walking and keeping them occupied. Jake was eager to buy clothes and furniture and had to be reminded they had most of the stuff already.

'I love this.' Jake said one evening as they played with Rose.

'Me too,' Silva said, 'but we still owe each other some dates.'

'Oh yeah? Where are you taking me? You should know I don't put out.'

'I have two pieces of evidence to say *yes you do*.' Silva laughed, rubbing her swollen stomach contentedly.

Jake laughed. 'I know where I'm taking *you* next.'

'Oh yeah? Where?'

'Surprise. Tomorrow night.'

'Okay,' Silva beamed, 'and yours is the week after.'

Jake's surprise for her turned out to be a musical in London. He had spied Silva playing her guitar for Rose more and more and asked if she had ever seen one – she hadn't.

They sat, laden with smuggled-in snacks from corner shops to avoid paying too much at the kiosk and Silva smiled at him. They watched Matilda the Musical together, and Silva fell in love with how the music worked with the story.

'I feel like I've done a weird swap.' She told Jake over a drink in a wine bar afterwards. She sipped her mocktail.

'What do you mean?'

'That show... it was like I left a bit of myself in there. But took another bit away. A new bit. A puzzle piece that fits better than the one I left.'

'I think you should write songs again. I like the way you describe things.'

'Maybe.' Silva said.

'I'm glad you liked it. That is what a good musical does to you.'

'Thank you for taking me.'

'Anytime. I think our weird little story would make a good musical.'

Silva smiled wistfully. 'I think people would think it was a weird watch.'

'Nothing is weirder than CATS.'

'Never seen it,' Silva reminded Jake.

'It's brilliantly awful. You have so much to learn,' Jake said, shaking his head, 'right. Let's get on the Tube soon. Work tomorrow...when is the weekend? I'm knackered.'

Silva raised an eyebrow. 'YOU are knackered? I'm carrying your spawn around.'

'I can be tired too, you don't have a monopoly.' Jake said, grinned and dodged a kick.

Jake hopped off his barstool to pay. Silva scrolled through her phone and tagged Liv in a funny post about grandmas and babies, her fingers tingling as she did so. It still felt strange – but nice – to have someone to tag. To have Jake. To be happy and settled, albeit exhausted and busy with work and mothering.

'Can we tell people yet?' Jake pleaded on the Tube home, his second glass of wine lightening his head.

'We only went official as a couple online the other day – it feels a bit soon. Plus, I'm not even 12 weeks yet – after that, please.'

'Okay. I just want to shout it all to the world. Ooh. Can we tell Layla?'

'Yes. We can tell Layla. Invite her and Opal over at the weekend and we can have a takeaway?' Silva said, unsure whether to blame her baby for the doner kebab craving that was driving her to distraction – or whether it was just being on the Tube after a night out, no matter how sober.

*

A few days later, Jake, Silva, Layla and Opal were all happily sat together playing board games and X-rated card games when they took a break for the arrival of food.

'How are things with you guys?' Silva asked, remembering to be a good host and friend while she filled her face with food.

'Busy! The café is doing well, which is good, the Saturday girls are now Sunday girls too but I need some full-timers.'

'And I'm good too. We are still looking for a permanent house, though.' Opal said.

'Ah, that's too bad. Did the other one fall through?'

'They took the bid of a first-time buyer. Rubbish.'

'The right one will come along.' Jake said. He refilled their glasses.

'How about you two?' Layla asked.

'We're okay. Busy at work – as you say, that's a good thing! Just tiring and Jake…'

'I'm cool. Work has been weird since I came back – I don't think anyone understands but it's fine. We do have some news, though… which must be a secret until Silva says otherwise…'

'Oooooh.' Layla said. 'I don't want to ruin it by guessing. Out with it!'

'I'm pregnant.' Silva said.

Layla's face was a picture of shock.

'Oh my goodness! Congratulations. What kind of magic sperm do you have, Jake?! I should have guessed… you're drinking coke. And eating a kebab…and your skin looks so nice.'

'How far along are you?' Opal asked.

'About 11 weeks. Scan next week to confirm.'

Layla counted weeks on their fingers.

'You dirty dogs got *right* to it. New Year was 11 weeks ago.'

'So it was.' Silva said, laughing. 'Don't judge me! It had been a while...it had been since... I GOT PREGNANT THE LAST TIME!'

'Have you guys not heard of condoms?' Layla asked.

'Oh, we have, for sure. But in the heat of the moment, we got carried away and ran out and we were irresponsible. Sorry, Mum.' Silva winked.

'On this occasion, I'll let you off.' Layla said, smiling. 'Jake, you make cute kids... you should definitely get some money for sperm donation,' they laughed.

Jake made a face. 'I can't afford to have them come for me asking for pocket money!'

'That's not how it works, idiot.' Layla said. Silva rolled her eyes. They ate and talked and laughed and everything felt right with the world.

*

A week later, Jake looked nervous as Silva lay back on the hospital bed and he held Rose up, who was taking in the sights and smells around her and babbling at the sonographer.

'Jake, it's going to be fine. It's just a check-up.' Silva said with more conviction than she felt. Her heart pounded. She wanted this moment to be perfect, a total parallel to when she had done this alone while pregnant with Rose. Jake shifted Rose's weight to squeeze Silva's hand. She smiled.

'I know...I just... I don't think it will feel real until I see the little bean on the screen.'

'Look at you, a poet and you didn't even know it.' Silva laughed.

Jake grinned. The sonographer squirted the cold goo onto Silva's stomach and rolled the machine over her. Silva flinched.

'Is she okay?' Jake asked.

'Yes, fine, it's just cold and hurts the full bladder a bit.' Silva assured him, although a warning would have been nice.

'So sorry, I had meant to pre-warn you. I have a lot on my

mind. Your little girl is adorable by the way.'

'Don't worry about it.' Silva said, as Jake beamed with pride and thanked her. Silva wanted to make the best of this, of having him there, his nervous optimism warming her heart. Rose chewed her hand, seeing her mother's soft belly out making her realise she was hungry.

The sonographer pointed out the small shape in the black and white grainy image of Silva's womb and Jake finally let a huge, happy smile escape, which matched Silva's. If he could have leant down to kiss her, he would have, but Rose would have got a mouthful of Silva's hair. They would have the photo to coo over later so neither minded all that much.

'Everything looks good, healthy at this stage.' The sonographer said. Rose started to gripe at Jake, who leant down, picked up a bottle from the insulated bag and shook it onto his wrist one-handed to check the temperature. Silva nodded her approval as she wiped the goo off her waist and went to be weighed and have other things checked. She grinned as she heard Rose try to snatch the bottle from Jake behind the curtain.

'You are a little above your ideal weight but nothing I would worry about. Looking at your last pregnancy, this is a huge improvement. Well done,' she said, her eyes kind.

'Thank you.' Silva said. 'I realised having someone to take care of meant I should have taken care of myself all along.'

'You'd be amazed how often I hear that.' The sonographer said. Silva finally read her name tag, *Julia*, and thanked her again personally before heading to collect her belongings and happy little family.

*

Several weeks later...

Silva was sat on her sofa playing with Rose when she felt something change in her body. She screamed at a sudden pain in her abdomen, frightened Rose and made her cry, somehow comforted her and made it to the bathroom for sanitary towels, as she felt heat and wetness, guessing correctly there was blood. She didn't have time to stop and give herself credit for thinking so clearly.

She grabbed her phone and sat on the tiled kitchen floor, letting Rose play in the living room where she could see her.

'JAKE?' Silva begged as he answered. 'Please come home. I need to go to the hospital. I'm... I'm bleeding.'

Jake's mouth went dry and his face went pale.

'I'll be right there.' He didn't remember the apologies he gave, packing up, logging off or driving home. Fear flashed over his eyes.

CHAPTER 16

'Silv? Oh, shit, Silv. I've got you.' Jake said, eyes wild with panic as he got home.

'Put Rose in her car seat – we can drop her to your mum on the way.' Silva said, level-headed enough to think logistically. Jake did as she said. Silva gingerly stood up from the kitchen floor, checking the tiles for blood. None. That was good.

Jake fumbled with Rose's car seat and tried to sing to her as he did so. She looked concerned and tearful.

'It'll be okay, Rosie Rose. I'm taking you to your Nanna's. She will look after you.'

Rose gurgled. Jake gave her a teething ring to gum on. She took it, bemused.

In a blur, they dropped Rose off to a pragmatically accepting Liv, and drove to the hospital.

'How do you feel?' Jake asked.

'I'm okay. I'm just worried.' Silva said. 'I feel like someone has burst the bubble and the bubble was me.'

Jake bit his lip, unsure what to make of that. He patted her leg for as long as he could before he had to change gear, hoping it helped her.

A&E felt like a long wait but in reality, they were triaged in ten minutes and seen in twenty. Silva ripped a tissue into snowy shreds. A man on crutches loudly complained as they got up when called.

'WHY DO THEY GET SEEN BEFORE ME? I'VE BEEN HERE HOURS, HOURS I'LL TELL YOU.'

'Because, mate, you're well enough to yell.' Jake muttered.

'He's not worth it.' Silva affirmed.

They sat in plastic chairs and told the doctor what was wrong. He tutted loudly.

'They should have sent you to maternity. Go now. Leave here, first right, then left, then right, then along the corridor, lift to the third floor, a right and then a left,' he said quickly.

'What do we say when we are there?' Jake asked.

'Tell them I sent you.'

'What's your name?'

The doctor sighed as if it was obvious and *everyone* knew his name. He wrote it down on scrap paper and they thanked him and left, then began trying to solve the labyrinth of the hospital.

'This is not stressful at ALL!' Silva remarked, both of them instantly forgetting all of the instructions the doctor had given them. Jake asked a nurse who was scuttling as fast as she could. She pointed them in the right direction. Two nurses and a few signs later, they had reached the ward.

'Ahh, why'd he send you here? You need early pregnancy... oh they closed at eight. Fine, take a seat...I'll get you seen quickly.' A brisk woman on reception said, her dyed scarlet curls gelled into a tight bun.

Silva and Jake sat, holding hands.

'I'm sorry that this is happening.' Silva said.

'Ssh. You don't know if *anything* is happening just now. and I'm here for everything. Not just the good bits. That's my kid in there too.'

Silva smiled at him weakly.

They were seen twenty minutes later. Silva explained her symptoms to a midwife, who nodded and sighed.

'You should have phoned ahead. They would have got you an appointment tomorrow.'

'I didn't know I could. I'm sorry. I didn't have anything like this with my first.' Silva explained.

'How much blood?'

Silva checked. The midwife peered but said nothing.

'Hop up here for me,' she said, more gently now, patting the blue-papered bed. Silva's heart started a heavy metal beat.

'Do you have a full bladder?'

Silva nodded.

She closed her eyes as the ultrasound jelly hit her little belly, trying her hardest not to cry.

A long moment passed, with Jake's hand holding hers, and the sound of plastic searching her stomach and digging in.

'There's a heartbeat,' the midwife said. 'You're twenty weeks – is that right?'

Silva released the breath that was holding her in place.

'Yeah.'

'I'm going to take your blood pressure and arrange some more tests.'

'Thank you.' Silva said. She took a deep breath as the midwife wrapped the Velcro sleeve on her arm and tried not to wince when it squeezed.

'We make babies easily, don't we?' Jake said as they sat with polystyrene cups of tea and waited for a blood test.

'What do you mean?'

'You got pregnant straight away both times we had sex for the first time.'

'Ha! Maybe we're just ultra-compatible. Jake used "impregnate"! It's super effective!'

Jake snorted with laughter. 'We are not Pokémon.'

'But who's to say we aren't?' Silva teased, feeling a bit lighter. She rubbed her belly, feeling the weirdness of someone being in there that she never quite got used to, even the second time around.

Jake grinned.

'Oh my goodness, Silva!' a voice said excitedly. A very pregnant Michelle waddled up to them in the waiting room and leaned down for a hug. Silva took a deep breath in and accepted.

'Hi, Michelle, nice to see you. Are you okay?'

'Yeah, just walking to try to get labour going. Can you believe I'm crazy enough to have done it again so soon?'

'No I can't! But then again....here I am too.' Silva said. 'How are you liking your new décor?'

'Still loving it. But never mind that, introduce me to this handsome fella. Where is Rose?'

'Sorry. Michelle, this is Jake. Dad to Rose and bump. Rose is with her nan.'

Michelle looked confused for a minute but smiled.

'Lovely to meet you. So, you don't seem far enough along for labour, is everything okay?'

Silva bit her lip. 'Jake, can you get us a hot chocolate please?' she asked. Jake nodded and dutifully got up.

'Just having some tests done... had a bleed.' Silva admitted, too scared to hold back and have Michelle at arm's length.

Michelle's hand flew to her mouth. 'Oh, hon.' She sat down and put her arm around Silva.

'Where's your husband?' Silva asked Michelle.

'I'm, erm... I'm doing this alone. And I'm so sorry if I ever made you feel bad for your doing it alone. How times have changed, hey.' Michelle said, her eyes strong and brave but full of tears. 'The secretary is more appealing than his children, his wife and his house. I'm keeping the house, luckily. Especially after you made it so beautiful.' Michelle said, beaming.

Silva smiled back. She saw a soft but tough side to Michelle that she hadn't before, past the "I'm perfect" façade to a mother primed and ready to do what she needed to do for her kids.

'I'm sorry about your husband. But if it's any consolation, I think you're going to do an amazing job of it alone.' Silva said.

'Thanks.' Michelle blushed, then took a few breaths through a contraction. She tapped her finger on her palm to count how long it was. Fifteen taps; fifteen seconds.

'Hey, Silv? Our kids are going to be so close in age. Don't be a stranger? I could use a genuine friend through all of this. He got our friends in the divorce proceedings.'

'Ah, that's awful. Of course, Michelle. I'd like that.' Silva said warmly.

Michelle smiled gratefully and started tapping her palm again. Jake returned with hot chocolate in Styrofoam cups and passed them one each.

'No but thank you, you drink it. I am going to hobble back to the bed now, I think the walk has done the trick, and seeing your lovely lady of course.' Michelle got up gingerly and started hobbling, groaning in pain as she did so.

'Jake, take her, will you?' Silva said as he looked at her, bewildered as to which pregnant woman he should help. 'I'll be all right for a few minutes.'

Jake nodded and took Michelle's arm. Silva watched them go, sipping a very watery hot chocolate that she didn't really want at all, and thought of how much nicer Michelle was when she had no airs and graces, and how that was the kind of friend she would need. Jake returned a few minutes later, having safely dispatched Michelle to her midwife and explained that no, he wasn't the father, just a helpful friend. He had barely sat down when the nurse called Silva in and took her blood. Jake came with her automatically. Silva thought for the second time how lovely it was to have him with her for this, how lonely it was the first time and how much scarier it would have been without him.

'You're all done. You'll need to come back in the morning please, for another blood pressure check. We should get your blood results by the end of the week. Oh, and you need this.' the nurse said, handing Silva a sample pot.

'Can I do that now?'

'I would say no, just because you had a bleed – do it tomorrow and bring it in after that so we can have a clearer picture please.'

'What are you testing me for?' she asked.

'A couple of things. I'm just here for the blood and the urine, you've got an appointment at ten tomorrow, come back and they'll talk to you about it. for now – go and get some sleep. Try not to worry. If there's something wrong, we'll do all we can to help you – but by all means, it might be nothing.' the nurse said. Silva spotted the weariness in her brown eyes but they were outshone by the kindness in them. Silva nodded, thanked her, and they left.

The next morning, after a troubled sleep, they went back to the hospital, waited, handed over a pot of wee, waited some more, had blood pressure tested, and left. The days were long and anxious until the appointment that told them what was wrong.

'Your tests are back from the hospital. You have preeclampsia.' The doctor said as they sat down in the GP surgery a few days later.

'And what does that mean…?' Jake asked.

'It means that Silva's blood pressure is high. She also has a low platelet count in her blood. Her urine came back fine. You're a little bit low on iron, but you should be able to fix that by including more of it in your diet. This, unfortunately puts you in the high-risk category and means that you may end up delivering early and in emergency circumstances. But we don't need to worry about that just yet. You are not a severe case but I would recommend that you do not undertake any strenuous physical activity from now on – and you buy a home blood pressure monitor. I'll give you some fact sheets on what to aim for and how to try to keep it lower. What do you do for work?'

'I run an interior design company – and I also fit and decorate within that also.'

'Is there desk work you can do?'

'I guess.' Silva said, bristling.

'I recommend you do it. I know it is difficult to change your pace. Gentle exercise is fine, though. Do you have other children?'

'A nearly one-year-old.'

'Try not to lift or carry your child…again, I will give you a leaflet. We will need to see you more. Your midwife will arrange appointments with you, and I will prescribe something for the platelets and some anti-hypertensives for the blood pressure that are safe for you. If you become severe, you may be at risk of seizures, so please take care of yourself.'

Jake rubbed Silva's leg as her face went white.

'Fuck.' Silva said as they left the surgery and made for the pharmacy. Jake steered her into the bakery first, and she paused her rant to select a doughnut for Rose and an iced bun for herself. 'I'm scared Jake. Really scared. I'm meant to just sit down for four months? I can't. I'll go crackers. Eric needs me, I...'

'I know. Eat your bun. You're too pale, I don't want you fainting. I think we've seen enough doctors for a week at least.'
Silva ate it and they walked into the pharmacy to hand in the prescription. Silva fiddled with a box of herbal iron supplements but none of the information stayed in her head. Jake gently took it from her, checked it was safe for pregnancy, and paid for it.

'I know it isn't going to be easy, Silv. But I promise you it won't be for long. I love you.'
Silva half-smiled at him. They went home. She took her meds and looked up ways to best deal with the illness, like a good patient but the sadness ate at her. After a few days, she went to bed in the afternoon while Rose was at nursery.

'They didn't prescribe complete bed rest.' Jake pointed out when he brought Rose home. 'Are you feeling okay?'

'Well, I'm not useful so I may as well wallow.' Silva said. Rose launched herself at her mother with the joy and speed of a newly- walking toddler and Jake winced and pulled her away. Silva's heart broke a little. 'Let her come in if she wants to.'
Jake sighed and nodded. Rose clambered into the bed.
Silva stayed in bed for the next couple of days, only moving for food, basic bathroom needs, or to the sofa to keep an eye on Rose. Jake scrambled to try to fix things – bought a TV and set it up in their room, bought her flowers, delivered food to her room, popped her meds into a pillbox and made sure she didn't need anything.
By the third day, he was exhausted himself. By the seventh, he called for backup.
Eric came first, sat on the boudoir armchair she had pilfered from a job when a client wanted to throw it in the skip.

'You're not here to tell me to come back to work, are you?'
Silva asked, eyebrow raised.

'I'm not your boss, honey, I'm your partner. You're going through some shit. It's fine to not be at work.'

'I just feel useless.'

'You are not at all. You are GREAT with the customers. You know how much I hate the admin. If anything, when you come back, you being on desk work will be a good break for ME.'

Silva swung at him from her bed but she laughed.

There was a knock on the door and Layla came in.

'Oh – hi – I don't want to disturb, I can wait with Jake and Rose...'

'No, more the merrier...nice to see you, Layla. It's been ages.'

'You too, mate. Silv.' Layla said, sitting on the bed. 'I've missed you. How are you?'

Silva sighed. 'You two should both be at work.'

'My love... your VERY SEXY MAN is worried about you. You described him as fit but my word, I could eat him with a spoon. His photos online don't do him justice...' Eric said. Silva laughed, knowing Jake would have heard that even if he was in the kitchen. Eric's voice was loud and the flat was small. 'He asked your two besties to come in to chat to you. See if we can make you feel better.'

'Yeah. Pretty much, Silv. Opal is absolutely fine. I left her with the baby group booking. If she's still broody after that, she's unshakeable. This is about you. Don't worry about Jake for now - although bless him, he looks knackered – just tell us what's on your mind. How we can help you.' Layla said, climbing into bed beside her.

Silva took a deep, deep breath. 'Fine, but please don't judge me.'

Layla nodded. Eric saluted her.

'I know I should be happy. My baby is safe. I'm in good hands, have good meds, we've got stable work that I can still do some of. I just feel every urge in me to run away somewhere... Spain to see my mum or something. Anything but reality, but the thought of doing so little for absolute *months*. I hate being told what to do. Jake is fantastic but so coddling – I think he's afraid to slap me out of it – but to be fair to him, I don't think I would take kindly to that either. I just feel so lost and frustrated... and urgh.'

'Silv... to be honest love, you're over halfway. I would have been talking to you about going desk-based soon anyway. I let you carry on too long last time. I love working with you – especially being out on jobs and seeing our designs come to life – but you can and will do that again, it's just that right now looking after yourself is more important. And I know you're stubborn about that. And if you want more manual work, you can be on coffee duty forever...'

Silva kicked him playfully in response.

'But seriously. You're cooking another mega-cute client magnet. You are doing *plenty* for our business. We can afford a new recruit, too – so I need you back when you're ready to hire one and do your scary interview face for whoever passes the paper sift.'

Silva smiled. 'Are we really that busy?'

'Silv...we are booked up until the end of the year!'

'Oh wow.' Silva frowned. 'That's great.'

'Yeah. That's why I need you in – handling that and out on jobs is knackering me – I have to dash off now as we have a client. But in the same vein, no pressure to come back until you feel better. The kettle is waiting for you.' he stood up and bent to hug Silva.

'Thanks, Eric.'

A few moments later, Layla took Silva's hand outside of the duvet and let her cry on their shoulder for a few minutes.

'Hey, hormones.' Layla said and kissed Silva's oily hair.

'Oh, goodness, I *hope* it's hormones. I can't bear feeling like this forever.'

'I'm sure it is. And new medicines. And the shock of it. Plus, as you say, you're *very* stubborn and don't like strict instructions.'

'Am I awful for feeling like this?'

'No! not at all. Remember how with Rose, you did it all on your own and you kind of got in your groove a bit. And you had to unlearn some of your ways when Jake came into your lives?'

'Yeah...'

'Well, it's a lot like that. You know your body can do it – yes, it's suffering a bit and needs you to be a bit stiller and sensible – but you aren't used to having the option to have someone else look after you, so you're kicking off a bit about it, I think. Perhaps don't view it as Jake is babying you – view it as he is helping you to grow the baby and if you both work together, neither of you will be as tired. And you need to find what that means for you – if it means you put Rose in nursery or with Liv or with us one day and go on a date with Jake, great, or time for yourself is great too. You still need to be a person and not a mum, an expectant mum, or a worker bee. You've never given yourself much downtime, Silv. For as long as I've known you, if you aren't working, you're learning something, out somewhere, always go-go-go. I've seen you take about four days of chill-on-the-sofa doing nothing in however many years it is now... you're owed some. Guilt-free. And if you wanna do that in bed, that's cool too. I know you desperately want to respond to your current ache with a grand adventure – your mother's is not the place to do that even if you could – but maybe you could take a long weekend with Jake somewhere you don't have to move much? It's getting warmer now – you could drive down to Cornwall, or Brighton, or something.'

'I would *love* a holiday.'

'Yeah! SEE? And you could go for strolls through little chocolate box villages, go shopping, go out for nice meals...'

'Why have we not thought of this before?'

'You aren't at my level of genius yet. Don't worry, it'll come.' Layla winked.

Silva laughed and sighed again. 'I just...had all my ducks in a row. Happy life – family going well... well, if you don't count my mum. Was really enjoying working...'

'I know. And you will again. Soon. Just first... enjoy yourself. Maybe start with a shower?'

'What are you saying?' Silva mock – gasped.

'That I feel better with clean hair and so will you.' Layla laughed. 'I have to go back to work too, but I'll check in on you soon.'

Silva nodded and accepted a hug. She gingerly got up at the same time Layla did, grabbed a fresh towel from the cupboard and followed Layla out.

Jake tried to hide his happy surprise at the sight of Silva stood up with intent when he said goodbye to Layla but Silva caught it and instantly felt guilty again. She showered, put fresh pyjamas on, and hugged him tight, her chest and shoulders tight with anxiety, and she thought Layla might be exactly right about them needing a holiday.

CHAPTER 17

'Don't you dare tell me to be careful.' Silva warned as she carried a full tray clinking with glasses to their table. Jake put his hands in the air.

'Consider me told.' he said, but he rescued a glass lemonade bottle before it fell and smashed. Silva winced.

Silva sat down in the sun, her bump almost making her too big for the garden armchairs of quite frankly the prettiest café she had ever been to – excluding Layla's of course. She closed her eyes and took a deep breath, letting Jake deal with giving Rose a sausage roll. She smiled at the hot sun on her face.

They had taken Layla's advice and were now on a last-minute holiday to a village in Norfolk that was full of old ladies who were delighted to see them. Off-season tourists with an adorable toddler in tow and such a lovely couple were such a treat for them that they had given them insider's tips on the best places to go – and they had all been spot on so far.

'Are you picturing an all-inclusive Caribbean resort?' Jake asked Silva as he watched Rose hold her sausage roll with her little finger up.

Silva thought for a minute. 'Actually, no. I don't want to be anywhere else but here right now.' as she said it, she realised it was the first time she ever had. A curious feeling of satisfaction settled over her hungry stomach.

'Me neither.' Jake said with a smile.

Rose broke the peace with a soggy – pastry sneeze that decorated the table and her parents. They laughed as they cleaned her up.

'Let's have a birthday party for Rose.' Jake suggested. 'It's come round fast. We can have it in Mum's garden, there's space for plenty of people, and it would be nice for our mums to meet...'

'If mine turns up.' Silva pointed out.

'-And a good chance to show people we're pregnant,' Jake said. 'I'm excited. I want to share that, even though it's a bit shaky and a bit scary still, but we are gonna be okay. Your mum will come.'

'People know,' Silva said, 'It's online. And I don't want the added pressure... or the work.'

'Yes it's online but I'm still excited and not everyone goes online. There is no pressure. I'll do the work. Nice people only.'

'Not sure why you've asked my mum then.' Silva grumbled, still sore from Joyce's lack of support during Rose's short life.

Jake shook his head. 'Maybe she just...is busy. Maybe you aren't always the easiest person to be around either – did you ask her for help? Did you invite her over?'
Silva narrowed her eyes at Jake and couldn't resist smiling.

'No, I suppose I didn't. But I wasn't raised to ask for help and I just presumed if she wanted to be involved, she would invite herself...I see other people online always with their mums and they are such involved grandparents and I just feel sad Rose doesn't have that with my mum – of course, I'm so happy to have Liv involved now...but...'

'And a lot of those people...do they rely on their parents for childcare?'

'Yeah.' Silva said.

'Well, that's probably why then... not everyone is as independent as you are, or have their own businesses that enable them to be flexible. A lot of them need nine to five childcare. And that means grandparents are now almost co-parents.'

'When did you get so clever?'

'I read a lot of parenting magazines in my lunch breaks.'

'Oh, Jake...' Silva said, speaking between breaths, laughing hard, 'that breaks my heart. You don't need those, and now you're spouting the crap in them back at me. Oh no, laughing hurts.'

Jake grinned and said, 'Failed to prepare is prepared to fail....'

'She's a child, not a fad diet. Come here, idiot.' Silva pulled him towards her and kissed him. 'You have a good point, even if it came from those ridiculous magazines, but I'm still not sure that my mum would give me help if I asked.'

'That'd be her loss, Silv. She'd miss out on you and Rose. She's already missed so much.'

Silva nodded. 'Okay. Let's have a party.'

'I knew you would come around.' Jake said.

*

A few weeks later, Silva took Rose to her birthday party in Liv's garden. She had let Jake get on with it; returning to work had her busy and Jake had promised to take on everything, and Silva wasn't sure what to expect.

'Wow.' she said as she let herself into the garden. Rose wrestled her pram for freedom and Silva unclipped her to allow her to walk over on her unsteady feet.

'You like it?' Jake appeared from nowhere, holding an enormous bunch of balloons.

'Yes... you have really gone for it haven't you?'

'My mum got overexcited too... loves a project.'

Silva had a proper look at the garden; tables set up, a huge cake covered by a bell jar, sandwiches and party food in cling film, balloons everywhere, a paddling pool, Layla and Opal furiously battling rainbow bunting while Eric filled party bags, and Liv emerging from her garden with Rose in a new bright pink party dress, closely followed by Reggie the enormous mongrel of a dog.

'I didn't even notice Rose was gone.' Silva laughed.

'She snuck into the house so I took the chance.' Liv said, smiling. 'You all right? I haven't seen you for a couple of weeks, you're looking well.' She said, kissing Silva on the cheek.

'Fine, thanks. This is amazing.'

'Good.' Liv beamed. 'Go put your feet up, I'll bring you my famous iced tea. Then I'll have the birthday girl inspect her party.' she said. Rose ducked her head shyly into Liv's neck. Silva smiled at her daughter.

'Are you sure I can't do anything?'

'No, sit.' Jake said, kissing her and then finding the perfect spot for the balloons. He ran to help Layla with the bunting straight after, as it got caught in her necklace.

'Am I late?' Silva heard a familiar voice say. She turned.

'Mum! Hi!'

'Hello darling, nice to see you. Look at you – so tanned. Beautiful.'

Silva hugged her mum in astonishment. She would never have bet she would have seen her turn up here in a thousand years.

'No Stefan?'

'No, he had to work. As usual... then again, this was all short notice, wasn't it? It looks fabulous though.'

'Yeah... Jake's idea.'

'Ah, Jake.' Joyce said, her eyes twinkling. 'No wonder Rose is such a pretty baby.' Joyce said loudly. Silva shook her head and her cheeks burned as Joyce marched up to him.

'Hello Jake.' Joyce said, smiling wide enough to show her teeth.

'So pleased to see you again. It's been a long time, thanks so much for coming.' Jake said sincerely, with his flirty lopsided grin. Silva shot him a glare over her mum's head.

'Pleasure to be here.' Joyce said, her tone softer. Silva wouldn't have been surprised to see her fluff her hair.

'Why don't you take a seat and catch up? I'll get you both an iced tea while we finish decorating.' Jake said, squeezing Silva's hand on his way out.

'He's a delight, isn't he?'

'Mum, you knew him when I was in school!'

'Yes, but he's grown up so much. I see why you love him. He's caring.'

Silva ground her teeth and scrunched her toes.

'So, are you staying with us, Mum?'

'Yes, love. Is that okay? Two nights then back home, Stefan

wants to take me for dinner for my forty-fifth birthday.'

'Erm… you turn fifty this year and in July.'

'He doesn't need to know that.'

'How old is he, Mum?'

'Thirty-three.'

Silva laughed and shook her head, accepting an iced tea from Jake.

'I can't wait to meet my new stepdad, I think we'll have a lot in common.'

'Behave now. He loves me, that's what matters.'

Silva nodded. Rose crawled up to her and used her mother's knees to pull herself up. Silva picked her up carefully and lifted her to her knee.

'Are you okay? You winced picking her up.'

'No, I'm just not meant to lift her. So I don't very often.'

'Why?'

'I have preeclampsia. So, no heavy lifting. Not too much stress. No manual work. Watch blood pressure…or end up on bed rest.'

'Is it definitely Jake's…?'

'Yes, it's Jake's. This time, with both of us sober. Still not planned, just a bit better prepared I suppose.'

Joyce laughed. She held her hands out for Rose, whose bottom lip quivered.

'You don't know me yet, do you? It's okay.' She said to Rose. Rose paused, looked at her grandmother and then leaned forward to be lifted. Joyce took her, bounced her on her knee and inhaled her hair deliberately and tenderly.

'I had high blood pressure with you. Felt rotten, always sick as a dog. That's why you have no siblings – I couldn't go through it again. They never diagnosed anything more than that, but after Barbara's girl got it, I think it probably was what you have.' Joyce said. 'It was awful. I'm sorry you're suffering.'

'They said it's rare to get it in the second pregnancy and not the first. I would rather have it in neither.' Silva nodded.

'Do you think you'll have more?'

160

'I don't know – my whole life is a pick and mix of surprises, I've given up planning.' Silva replied, scratching Reggie's chin.

Joyce laughed. 'You're wise.'

A moment of silence passed as Rose relaxed into her grandmother's hair-stroking. Silva smiled. She knew how calming those hands could be, and unwelcome, sour thoughts came into her head. *Why are you here now? You've missed so much of Rose's life, my life. You abandoned me for Spain.*

Silva took a long sip of her iced tea. Was it pregnancy hormones or was she genuinely angry? Could it be both?

Jake sat down at their table, wiping sweat off his forehead with his palm.

'You two all right?' he asked.

'Great, thank you.' Joyce answered. 'The party is looking wonderful.'

'Thanks.' Jake said. 'People will be here soon... Rose, you've got guests to entertain, you can't nap.' he said, chuckling fondly. Rose smiled at him sleepily.

'She had a good sleep, she probably won't.' Silva said. 'But it's so hot that I could use a nap.'

'Go and lay down in the spare room, if you want, Silv,' Jake said. 'Mum won't mind.'

'I might just do that.' Silva agreed and got up. 'Come get me soon though, I don't want to miss too much.'

Silva lay down and was asleep in moments. She woke to the feeling of soft hands lifting her feet onto a pillow.

'Sorry, love. Don't wake up. Your ankles were swollen, I thought this would help.'

'It's okay, Mum. What time is it?'

'You've only been out half an hour. I wanted to look in to make sure you didn't need anything.'

'Nah,' Silva said. 'Just my mum,' she said softly. Joyce sat on the edge of the bed and stroked her daughter's hair.

'I know. I'm sorry,' Joyce said. 'I've not been the best, have I? I'm sorry. It's been tough the last few years, your dad... I needed to get away. And you were always so independent, that I

161

thought you would be fine. You're okay, right? You've been okay?'

Silva sighed deeply. 'Not always. It was so much harder feeling like I was alone. Sometimes I felt like I'd lost two parents.'

Joyce bit her lip. 'I'm so sorry.'

'I don't mean to be accusatory, Mum. I know it was hard for you too. I would probably have done the same or similar. And really, you anchoring me by making me take on a mortgage was probably a good thing. I grew up and learned about real life, but my word it was tough, and then Rose... I could really have benefitted from your help.'

'I wish you had asked or said something. I felt you didn't want or need me. You and Layla just seemed to have things sorted. I figured if you wanted me to help you, you'd have asked and then I would have come back.' Joyce said, sniffing back tears.

'I would never have presumed you would drop your life and move for me. I wish you had offered to be around more, Mum. Rose would love to get to know you more.' Silva grabbed them a tissue each from the box on the bedside table.

'What a pair we are, hey. Takes you being hormonally charged up and me being in the same room for us to talk properly.' Joyce said.

'Yeah.' Silva blew her nose. 'Will you come and see us more often? Hang out with the kids?'

'Only if you promise to come and stay sometimes too. The kids will love the beaches.'

Silva smiled at the thought. 'Yes, deal.' They hugged. 'Now – shall we go outside and say hello to some people? Get some food?' Silva asked.

'Sounds good to me. You have some news to share – Jake is dying to tell the world you're pregnant but wants you there. Not that it's hide-able anymore anyway. He's a keeper.'

'I know. I'm very lucky.' Silva said. Joyce took her daughter's hand and led her outside, both of them smiling, and they spent a happy afternoon surrounded by love.

'Are you okay? Do you still feel low?' Jake asked a few days after the party, and they had put Rose to bed and got the flat back in order after Joyce had gone home.

'Yeah. I'm okay. I have sad days – I always will have, I think, pregnant or not. And that's okay. That is just my mind, I suppose. But right now, I'm good. I see what I have – how lucky I am. And I also see I can be so stubborn and my brain feels like it's been scrunched into a paper ball sometimes and I kick off and then... you or Layla or Eric will do or say something and I realise I'm not alone.'

Jake rubbed a hand softly over her belly and bent to kiss it.

'You'll never be alone. You have children,' he teased. Silva grinned back.

'I just... I've been thinking a lot. I remember being worried that I would be "just" a mum when I first found out I was pregnant. I don't think I had the best role model...I felt like nothing but a burden to my mum – well, more an obligation she has to check in on. I never want that for our kids. I never want to be distant. I always want to know what's going on with them. Now I think that "mum" might be my favourite part of myself.'

'You're cute sometimes.'

'I know.' Silva winked and switched the TV on. She woke up later, the TV still blaring on, but Jake was fast asleep next to her. She rubbed her leg to wake up the pins and needles and felt something solid and not leg related. She pulled it. Jake's phone was in her hands. Vibrating with a phone call and a picture of a magazine-cover woman who was saved as "Meg". Her hands shook. She silenced the call but let it ring out, head pounding in confusion, part of her brain ringing alarm bells about her blood pressure but she ignored it, and checking that Jake was still asleep, she checked his notifications. Piles of messages from Meg asking where Jake was, why he wasn't replying, and that she loved him.

Silva's heart caught in her throat.

CHAPTER 18

Silva stared at her sleeping boyfriend, realising how much she had let him in. How hard she had worked on trust and vulnerability, and now this. She resisted the urge to hit him and stood up, letting his body flop hard on the sofa, and went to bed. She left the phone on the sofa with him instead of smashing it to bits.

She cried herself to sleep, half of her brain fighting that there was a logical explanation, the other half chanting *I told you so.*

Silva woke up when he came to bed, when Rose fussed next door, and then she tossed and turned.

'I really could have done with a better sleep than that.' She growled to herself as she made a coffee and washed Rose. The moment Jake got up, she ran for the shower so Rose wasn't unattended.

'Are you okay? You're a bit off.' Jake questioned as she came into the living room, running finger curls through her hair.

'Uh-huh. Fine. I'm going to the office. I'll drop Rose to your mum on my way?'

'I'll do it. She wants me to put something up anyway. Plus. It's only 7?'

'It's a big day, Jake. I want to be in early to make sure we have everything sorted for a job's "after" pictures, we've got another commercial client in to discuss designs, and I need to stock up the office fridge...'

'Okay. have a good day.' He said, looking troubled.

Silva made it to work with a bag of pity-pastries and Eric grinned at her.

'I love you most when you're pregnant, you get the best

food,' he said.

'I have never not gotten good food!' she protested.

'I didn't say that. You just get a bit more *extra* when you're preggo. I apologise.'

Silva breathed out. 'Sorry. I shouldn't have snapped,'

'No worries, Silv. Right. I've got a bit of a surprise for you, so prepare your blood pressure.'

'I'm not sure it can take much more.' Silva said with a half-smile.

'What's happened?' Eric asked her softly, and she burst into tears and told him through snotty, choked sobs.

'What a prick.' Eric whistled. 'He has brought shame onto all the fit men.'

'I know, right.'

'You need to talk to him about it, though. You can't just let it slide.'

'Yeah. But my hormones are raging. I can't even look at him without wanting to hurt him, and for the sake of a clean criminal record and not becoming a domestic abuser, I just think coming to work will do for now,' she said with a sigh as she composed herself.

'Well, I have good news at least. The corporate project you designed – that absolutely stunning one for the Purbow client – is finished. And they love it so much they want to show it off – even on TV, they have connections, and a magazine feature. They will probably want photos and interviews...so get down the hairdresser.' Eric winked.

'That's amazing! What a compliment.' Silva said happily.

'Next bit of news...their contact is coming in later today to discuss exclusive designs for one of their buddies. Could be BIG.'

'Oh, wow,.' Silva said with a grin. She chomped on a pastry and wondered if she should go home and put some make-up on, but rejected the idea before it formed properly. 'That's fantastic.'

'Oh – and my last thing. I'm moving in with Layla and Opal.'

'You what?!' Silva said, bemused. 'How did this come

about?!'

'Well, we saw each other when we were comforting you out of your bed of despair.'

'I prefer to call it, "my growing space", but continue.'

'And we went for a drink after we finished work, just to agree to kind of... keep an eye on you, and we spoke about how much we both loved you and how mad it is we never really hang out other than at Christmas, and she got talking about how she and Opal had found a place they love but were having trouble affording the mortgage, and I mentioned my lease was coming up and how much I hate my flat...and it just kind of clicked. They do buy-to-let. I move in and rent at a low fee to save for a place and help them do theirs up. Be with nice housemates. What could be better?'

'Lesbians work fast even on gay men.' Silva said, and Eric laughed. 'I expect many, many parties.' Silva said with a smile. Eric nodded his agreement.

They set to work, Eric heading out to check the progress of a couple of jobs. Silva watched him go with the residual stab of sadness that she couldn't go too, but today it was less pronounced. They were doing well. She finished emailing and calling clients, made a coffee and cleaned the kitchen.

'Hello?' a voice called.

'Hello, one second.' Silva called back and went out to their little reception space.

'My name is Bob Karen. PR director for the Purbow estate. I don't believe we have met. Eric asked me to come in today to discuss a new client of mine with you.'

'He said you would be coming, welcome! I'm so pleased you liked our work. Can I get you a drink? He should be back very shortly.'

'I'd love a tea. One lump, not much milk, please.'

'Coming right up. Please make yourself at home.'

Silva made the tea, pleased she had bought decent biscuits instead of lovely – but not quite appropriate for a potentially huge client – custard creams. She set the plate down in front of Bob as

Eric came in, paint-covered and grinning.

'Oh, good, you're here. I've made you a coffee, come sit down.' Silva said.

'Brilliant.' Eric said, too excited to admit he was desperate for the toilet.

'Thank you for meeting with us.' Eric said to Bob. 'We're excited to have you here. What did you have in mind?'

'Straight to business, I like that in a man.'

'Sorry, I should have asked how you were.' Eric blushed.

'Not at all, not at all. So, I have been in touch with my features editor for *Spotlight*, and he will be contacting you shortly, and I have left a message with the producers of *Incredible Homes*.'

'Wow - what a fantastic opportunity!' Silva said.

'Well deserved. You've made my client incredibly happy, and any way in which we can both give him some excellent exposure and help your business seems a good idea to me.'

Eric nodded. 'We have a bit of a time constraint for interviews as Silva here is seven months pregnant...'

'But I have childcare if needed, I can be flexible.'

'Of course. It's normally a couple of weeks' wait for magazines and then around two months till they publish, but we are hoping to get a bit of a rush on that as Mr Purbow has an album and a tour to be released, and would like to invite the press sooner rather than later. As for the TV, I can't confirm I'm afraid but a family included in the shots of you wouldn't hurt your image. Sells the "small family business" vibe.'

'We aren't together.' Eric said.

'Bit too quick to reject me there, Eric.' Silva laughed.

'I had kind of guessed that,' Bob said. Eric blushed. 'I mean that you,' he directed his point to Silva, '- have a small family. And that your co-director is gloriously gay.'

Eric relaxed. Silva smirked a bit. She wondered if Eric could tell he was being flirted with, what he thought of this handsome older, rich gentleman who had a twinkle in his eye and a kind nature. She liked the idea of them together.

'I think WE need you as OUR PR.' Eric said.

'You can't afford me.' Bob said, grinning.

'So, you wanted to talk about designs for another project?' Silva asked instead of asking if she should leave them to their flirting.

'Oh, yes, a hotel design; a client of mine is keen to expand his portfolio, and I showed him your designs and website, he ADORED them. He would love you to design his hotel interior and rooms; he has ideas for themes; there are 200 rooms but not all of them would be unique- general colour schemes/themes but several of them. He is on a large budget and is willing to pay you well if he does take on your designs... are you interested?'

'Wow. Yes, of course we are! What is the theme?'

'It's "Around the world." He wants tasteful designs inspired by different countries to reflect his love of travel. He would like it to be subtle enough not to be gimmicky, but obvious enough to make people feel like they step through the hallway and into that country.'

'This is my dream,' Silva said wistfully. 'How is he doing the corridors? *Please* don't say bad carpet and magnolia walls. I'll cry.'

'HA! I know exactly what you're saying. No. Please look through the brief, which includes corridors and reception space, I believe.'

'Do we have a deadline?'

'He would love to see designs in a month, ideally. The hotel is going through planning permission at the moment.'

'Excellent. We can do that.' Silva said with excited confidence, despite knowing how full their workload was.

'I have to head off to another meeting, so I won't take any more of your time, but I'll be in touch.'

'Thank you.' Silva beamed. Eric shook his hand and walked him out while Silva ran to the loo, her heart beating fast, happily, but she worried about how hard it was beating and about the baby. She took some deep breaths.

'SILV!!!!'

'I KNOW!' she said excitedly, ruining her attempts at

calming.

'No that too but I'VE BEEN BUSTING FOR HOURS GET OUT OF THERE!'

Silva laughed and came out of the loo.

'We're going to need a third designer at this rate.' Silva said a few minutes later as they stopped for a late lunch.

'That might not be a bad idea, y'know.' Eric agreed. 'I'm exhausted, man. And we still have another meeting.'

'YOU'RE exhausted.' Silva laughed.

'Self-inflicted, hun.' he said and rolled his eyes. She kicked him affectionately under the table.

'And maybe a nicer office. One that we can decorate a bit more. And a receptionist to answer emails…'

'Let's look at the finances before we get too far ahead of ourselves. But I LOVE the thoughts. We've done well. Telly and lots of press, two kids and countless homes and offices revamped. And I am about to live as a third wheel with Netflix as my boyfriend. I'm proud of us.'

'Me too.' Silva said.

A client's face peered round the door. Eric swallowed his mouthful and welcomed them in.

'So, what we are looking for is sleek, sophisticated designs for our open-plan offices.' Dave, their corporate client told them a few minutes later. Silva heard: *we want everything in grey tones, silver if we're feeling decadent,* but she nodded along and made notes. It would be easy but boring. There was nothing wrong with that as a money earner, she supposed.

'Fantastic. How would you feel about a dash of colour – yellow, or perhaps red? We have some really beautiful, chic furniture stockists. I can let you nose through the catalogue if you'd like?'

'Err, I will have to suggest it to them, they are keen on the idea of sleek…'

'Not a worry. Take all the time you need and let us know.' Eric said. 'We are happy to take your job on, please do send us an email when your colour scheme and furniture requirements are finalised and we'll send some ideas... also feel free to come back and look through our magazines and portfolios anytime. We will book confirm dates when you know. Anything else I can help with today?'

'Can I take a business card for my friend?'

'Please do – take a few if you'd like to!' Eric replied.

'Thank you.'

'Fantastic to meet you.' Silva chipped in before walking him out and wishing him a good day. 'Well that was exciting,' she said as she dried the cups Eric had washed up.

'Ssh, you. Not everyone wants a rainbow office. Besides. All jobs are now going to pale in comparison to A WORLD THEMED HOTEL.' He put them away in their cupboards.

'You're right.' Silva grinned. She checked the time. 4 pm. 'Right. I'm going home.'

'Me, too. Got to start packing my stuff.'

'You better invite me over when you're settled in.'

'Obvs.' Eric agreed as he switched off lights and locked up behind them.

In the car, Silva's stomach turned over as the excitement of the day wore off and she drove to collect Rose, remembering Jake and the messages from another woman. Would the conversation they had that evening ruin their relationship? *If it does,* she reminded herself, *it won't be my fault.*

She accepted a cup of tea from Liv as Rose carried on watching her film. *Anything to avoid going home yet.* Silva thought. She hadn't sent Jake a message all day, other than to let him know she would fetch Rose. She thought of Michelle, wondered if she should ask if she was overreacting, but didn't want to worry her. She was busy enough with baby Frank, who Silva had cuddled a couple of days before and fallen in love with.

Jake was home when Silva returned, the smell of mushrooms and beef permeating the flat. Silva's stomach rumbled despite her anger. She set Rose down to run to him and busied herself setting up a game for Rose to play to distract her from what would happen next. Jake put Rose down and she toddle-ran over to what Silva had set up and clapped her hands. Silva smiled and stepped into the kitchen.

'Who is Meg?' she asked when Rose was properly absorbed.

'My ex from a while back.' Jake replied.

'What was she doing calling and texting you last night? Saying she loved you?'

Jake went a bit pale. 'She was drunk, Silv. She didn't realise we were together and thought she could booty call me.'

'She didn't check you out online then. And what did you say? Did you call her back?'

'I text her back saying that I'm not available.'

'Can I see?'

Jake went from ghost-white to lobster-red in his cheeks.

'I deleted it all. I didn't want to see it again.'

Silva sighed. 'That seems suspicious...'

'I didn't realise you had seen anything.' Jake snapped. 'You didn't say anything. Do you not trust me? Why didn't you say you'd seen it?'

Now it was Silva's turn to flush. 'I didn't go looking. Your phone woke me up and I only saw what she was typing from your lock screen. But you might have a point. Maybe I should have woken you up and seen what you did about it then?'

'She's gone, Silv. What do you want me to say to you? If I didn't love you, I wouldn't be with you.'

'Jake, my last ex cheated. I'm scared. You aren't exactly known as the settling-down type. She is a fucking supermodel or may as well be. Don't be a dick. Just tell me the truth right now. And block her. And tell me if she messages you again. Or leave. I can't have my trust wrecked again.'

'I'll block her, Silv.' Jake said. 'Honestly - I'm not even friends with her anymore. She was just drunk and horny. Please just try to calm down, your blood pressure...'

'Shut up about my bloody blood pressure.'

'Okay. Look. Number blocked and deleted.' Jake showed

Silva as he removed Meg from his life.

'Thank you. It means a lot.' Silva said, letting out an enormous breath of relief.

'I wish you had just spoken to me earlier rather than stewed on it.' Jake said.

'Sorry. Old habits die hard. I just thought I was about to lose you. I was scared.' Silva replied. 'How was work?' she said, accepting his hug.

'Fine, thanks. Boring. Inspired me to make...this experiment.'

'Chaos smells nice.' Silva said as she looked at the pans and dishes.

'Why thank you. how was *your* day?'

'Good! Busy. We're talking about getting another designer in as work keeps picking up and obviously, I'll be a bit limited in how much I can help,' Silva said, rubbing her stomach. 'A client wants us to design a whole hotel. World themed.'

'That sounds exciting!'

'SO exciting! I want to get started now. Do you think we can reschedule the hospital so I can go in tomorrow?'

'No! You have to go. We are taking Rose to the aquarium afterwards. It's going to be a nice day. No work.'

Silva put out her lower lip but grinned, 'I know. I'm going to sit down. Feed me soon.' she said. She kissed him before sinking into the sofa. Rose abandoned her game of mashing plastic boxes together loudly to disturb Silva's peace and use her face as a toy, but she didn't mind. She pretended to chew Rose's fingers, who laughed in her high–pitched squeak.

*

The next day, the hospital visit was completely fine and both of them let out a sigh of relief. The medications and changes to active life were working. Silva felt less sad about dropping manual work because of it. The midwife cooed over Rose and gave her a sticker. 'It doesn't matter if she eats it. It's made of natural stuff.' she explained as Silva watched her child instantly begin peeling it off her dress and went to stop her.

Later, when they were home from the aquarium, Silva got a phone call from Eric.

'How was it today?'

'Well, I missed you. but it was okay, not much to report for AT work...'

'So what about NOT at work?'

'Well, Bob and I had a chat last night.'

'Oo-er, outside office hours?'

'Yep... he wanted a chat. Anyway...he's great but he forgot to mention something in our meeting.'

'What's that?'

'The hotel is in Italy. And he wants us there to oversee everything. All expenses included, and family too.'
Silva's jaw dropped.

CHAPTER 19

Silva hung up the phone, bemused. It felt too soon after one serious conversation with Jake to have another. Luckily, Jake didn't ask. He was busy playing with Rose at that moment and she was grateful for that.

Italy. Wow.

The simple answer was that she could just…not go. Look after baby and business at home. The design would be done before she gave birth, but planning permissions could take months, so actual work done out there… it could be a while before they were ready to put them up anyway.

The more complicated answer was to go, enjoy the beautiful sunshine, amazing food, maybe learn a new language at the same time…and uproot her little family completely.

Including Jake and his job… Silva thought. She chewed her lip and put the kettle on.

*

Silva did what any sensible heavily pregnant person would do and ignored the problem for a few weeks, choosing instead to anxiously eat chocolate while she tried to enjoy the time she could – when she wasn't horribly uncomfortable and shifting position every few minutes to try to find ten seconds where she didn't feel as heavy as the whole world.

'You could go into labour at any time, and you will need to get here as soon as possible when you do,' her midwife had told her on her last visit. 'But everything still looks okay. Are you staying out of trouble?'

'Well, you know. Kind of.' Silva laughed nervously. 'I'm not working as much now. A couple of days a week, admin only.'

The midwife rolled her eyes. Jake laughed at her. She had to tell him. She would tell him. What was she afraid of?

Not going, I guess, she answered herself.

'Everything is sore,' Silva complained to Layla over the phone on one of her days off. Rose was with Liv and Silva felt more lonely than relaxed. 'Why did I do this again?'

Layla laughed. 'Because you love having babies. You know the uncomfortableness won't last forever. Soon, you will have a tiny being dependent on you for everything and you'll find that *far* more annoying.'

'Ha-ha. But, true. I still loved Rose needing me that much, as much as it drove me mad.'

'That's it. Motherhood. Constantly battling between your need to nurture and the want to run away and have a child-free existence.'

'You get me. You always get me.' Silva laughed, rubbing her stomach.

'But it's all worth it, though, isn't it?' Layla asked, a strange edge in her voice.

'Don't worry Layla, it's all completely worth it. I don't regret anything. I'm not going to leg it and leave you with them.'

Layla laughed down the phone. 'Good. Now, go have a lie-down. Enjoy your alone time, there'll be no more of that in a few weeks. I'll see you soon.'

Silva woke up to Jake slamming the door. She took some deep breaths, conscious of her heart rate and its mini in-utero echo.

'Jake?' she shouted hopefully. He walked into the bedroom and let out a deep sigh. 'Hey. Get in here.' Silva said, patting the bed. Jake obliged. Faceplanting the pillows, he let out a soft moan as Silva rubbed his back.

'What's up, Jake?' she asked, lifting his shirt to rub his rigid shoulders.

Jake took a deep breath and felt immensely grateful and ashamed all at once. He rolled to his side and let his hands rest on Silva's bump.

'I'm okay. I just...is this adulting? A permanently messy kitchen, a job you kind of hate, feel trapped in, and living for the hours of the evening and weekend where we get to be a family all together? Is that all life is?'

Silva bit her lip and tried not to let his words sting.

'I'm sorry about the kitchen, I...'

'That's not what I mean. It's not about the kitchen. Besides, remember all the time I left yours in a state! You're meant to be resting. I just...'

'Have you had a bad day?'

'Stressful, yeah. Trying to tutor the newbie is like pulling teeth. She doesn't want to learn, and we can't get rid of her without giving her a fair chance and it's just hell. No one else will try to train her.'

'Oh, no. You should refuse!'

'I've tried, they upped my pay for the tutoring period to keep me doing it and I...'

'Am a sucker for a few extra quid.' Silva finished for him.

'Yeah.' Jake said and grinned in spite of himself. 'We just... dreamed of more, didn't we, as teenagers?' he said, searching her face for something.

Silva smiled. 'This isn't quite the rock star dream I had planned at seventeen, no. But that's my choice and I love it. I'm happy. And if you really hate your job... change it. Life is too short to dread Mondays and while Rose and I – and whoever is in here...' she patted her stomach, '...are definitely excellent weekend and evening company, you should enjoy work at least sometimes too.'

Jake nodded and yawned. 'You're right, Silv.'

'Always am. Right. I am sick of these four walls and I think we should go somewhere nice seeing as your mum has Rose tonight...how about Italian? My treat?' Silva said, a plan forming in her mind. 'We can dress up a bit. I for one would love to feel human again for a few hours. Come on.'

Jake smiled. 'Okay. That sounds nice...no cooking... if I clean the kitchen it will *stay* clean for a few hours. That's the adulting dream.'

'I solemnly swear it will stay clean until your daughter comes home. After that, I take no responsibility for that or the rest of the flat.'

Jake laughed and leant to kiss Silva, and then her bump.

'Deal. Maybe I'll take a photo to remember it by.'

Silva rolled her eyes. 'Get up... it's time to get ready. I'm hungry.'

Later, after their starters had been taken away and Jake was enjoying his white wine, Silva took a deep breath.

'Jake, I need to tell you something.'

'Go for it.'

'That hotel design Eric and I are doing...it's in Italy.'

'Wow, international. That is cool!'

'It is.' Silva took a moment to appreciate the fact, as in her fear and worry and drive to do the job she had forgotten to celebrate it. 'The issue is...well I suppose it's not really an issue. More of a...I don't know. They want us to move out there for the implementation. They want our team. All expenses and family included.'

Their main course arrived. They thanked the waitress.

'Is this why we're eating Italian right now?'

'I can neither confirm nor deny,' Silva said, nodding and laughing.

Jake played with his tagliatelle. 'It would be amazing. And a nice escape.'

'Yeah, it would.' Silva agreed. 'But it's a big change. Don't get me wrong – it would be a few months away yet. I think about... three or four months. They need to time it so the install can be done in the quiet season – after Christmas, before Spring.

'Is Eric going?'

'Of course he's going. He was going before the dude had finished asking him the question. Of course. There is the option for me to stay. Look after things here. I'm sure they would under-stand and just have Eric. But...can we think about it?'

'Of course. I just...uh...I've been offered something too.

177

Really good money. Managing a team in L.A. They asked just after they sweet-talked me into not quitting the tutoring.'

'America again?!'

'Yeah. But this time...with you and the kids. Relocation costs. Subsidised accommodation in the city, guaranteed places for schools...permanent. Well, a five-year contract. You wouldn't need to work anymore, Silv. The money is that good. We could buy a place out there. There's Disneyland about an hour or so away...'

'Oh, wow.' Silva said. Her heart did a disco beat. 'Typical. As soon as I feel happy staying still for the first time in my life, here we are!'

'We don't have to make any decisions right this moment.'

'True. Do you have a deadline?'

'They're giving me until your due date. You?'

'No pressure then,' Silva said sarcastically. 'No deadline as such, but I imagine they will want us to talk it over when we submit the final designs to them next week.'

'Okay.' Jake said simply.

'So, was it really that newbie you were stressed about?'

'Partially, yeah. But it was this that was stressing me too. It's all at once and I just didn't know what to do. Thank you for taking me out.'

Silva tried to ignore the knot of anxiety that was tangling itself in her stomach but it persisted, her brain feeding it panic. *Our lives are here, our dreams are here, and coming true...and now he wants to go all the way across the sea and start again. As fun as L.A. might be it isn't kid-friendly, and I've heard it's full of mega-thin people obsessed with staying mega-thin, and I don't want to bring my kids up like that, and how BORED would I be as a housewife? Then again, how cool would it be to be interior designer to celebrities? Eric would love to visit. Oh, Eric. What would he do in this situation? How would he feel if we went to LA and not Italy?*

'Are you okay in there?' Jake asked her, finishing his plate.

Silva looked down and shook her head to put better thoughts in there: cheesy chicken. Much better.

'Yeah. Busy brain.' Silva said. 'I could *really* use a gin and tonic.'

'Not long until you can have one.' Jake said. 'Don't freak out. We'll work this out. Together.'

Silva nodded and finished her food. After a while, they shared a huge tiramisu sundae for dessert, and having a stomach full of comforting food made her feel slightly better – or at least, a bit number to her exhausting brain. The discussion continued once they were home.

'What do you think we should do?' Silva asked. Jake sighed.

'I don't know, Silv. Both would be pretty amazing places to live in their own ways, and both have challenges. America is a scary place with guns and stuff but I really liked it when I was there. Italy is also a bit scary... I've heard there's mafia in certain places, you know... everywhere has things about it.'

'True. Some people are scared to move *here* because people get stabbed.' Silva pointed out. 'They fail to remember that it's usually over drugs and territory.'

'Exactly. And I don't think we would get in that sort of trouble.' Jake laughed. He made them a hot chocolate each as Silva leant against the kitchen door frame.

'You say that. There isn't a baby in here. This is a few hundred kilos of heroin.' Silva laughed.

'Well, the midwives are in on it too huh? Do I get a cut?'

'Only if you're nice to me.' she countered.

They said no more about their decisions but it was all either could think about.

The next day, in the office, Silva told Eric about their chat.

'You only JUST had this chat? I told Layla and Opal that night!'

'Yes Eric, but you hadn't only just had a trust wobble with them about possible cheating and didn't feel too fragile at the time, did you? And if you remember I've got to keep the stress levels low. So yeah, it took until last night. And then he comes out with that....'

'Sorry. It's an odd situation to be in, poppet. Of course, I want you to be happy and if that means you go off to America then the suitcase better be big enough for me.' He laughed. 'I can deal with things here if that's what you decide to do. I will buy you out eventually...if that's what you decide. But what are you thinking about it?'

'You ditched me quickly!'

'I just don't want you to worry. I don't *want* you to abandon me. But this isn't about me.'

'I'm thinking... America is a long way to go but Jake already stunted his career for me once this year. It would be selfish to stop him. But I kind of don't want to go and, I kind of do. I just don't fucking know, Eric, and I'm so tired.'

'You're allowed, mate. You're a million years pregnant.'

'Rude.'

'Lunch delivery for my favourites.' Layla shouted as they came into the office. 'I know it's early. They're best after half a minute in the microwave to get them good and melty. I'm busy today. Hi, Silv. Are you okay?'

'You know me, babe. Always some sort of existential crisis. Today we are visiting; which country should I move my family to? Which of our careers do we follow?'

'Yikes.' Layla said, sitting down. Eric popped up and put the kettle on. 'I have fifteen minutes before my next delivery is due and it's only around the corner from the shop. Tell me everything.'

Silva did. Layla nodded throughout.

'Never boring with you, is it?' they said finally. 'I'll really, really miss you if you go to either Italy America but we will visit. You have to do what is best by you, yeah, but also really...what's best for the kids.'

'Speaking of,' Eric said, 'have you booked your tests in Layla?'

Layla blushed. Eric looked panicked.

'What's this about?' Silva asked.

'We...Eric, Opal and I, are looking into having a baby together. Co-parented.'

'I knew you got on well but didn't know THIS well?' Silva said, mouth open in shock. 'I think I might end up in labour at this rate!'

'Nooo, not yet. I – we weren't saying anything yet in case there was medical stuff that would stop us. But Eric and his big mouth...'

'Sorry.'

Layla grinned. 'It's your fault, Silv. Rose made us broody. Opal's marriage broke up as she couldn't have kids, and he decided by "infertile" she had said "let's fuck other people". We thought it would be a good fit. Have a baby with an unconventional parentage. Make it work around work. We had seen it done. By you.'

'I'm pleased, I think?' Silva laughed. 'And you have an extra person. And me to help you. This is cool! It'll be the most wanted baby in the world. And the cutest. I guess that means you're carrying?'

'Yeah, me. I feel weird about it, but it'll be fine, right?

'Yeah, just don't think about the constant peeing, muscle aches, constipation, swollen ankles or what it does to your teeth, and it's a dream.' Silva said with a wink. 'What about Bob?' Silva asked Eric.

'That's very early days yet,' he blushed. 'He will have to love me AND my kid.' He puffed his chest out and flicked an imaginary lock of hair out of his face dramatically.

'You guessed too?' Layla said.

'He's subtle as a brick through a glass window,' Silva chuckled.

Layla laughed. 'Right. More lunch deliveries,' they said, checking their schedule.

'When did you start delivering?'

'Piloted this week. Eric kindly was my first order for the both of you. Added in a cookie each because I'm nice like that.'

'So nice, I'm so proud!'

'See, this is what you would miss if you went to America.'

'Yeah, but think of my leaving party. You could get pregnant manually in the toilet.' Silva said dryly.

Eric and Layla looked at each other and laughed.

'We're good with the turkey baster and the good old-fashioned baby boomer parenting method of feeling disgusted physically by the other, but with the modern twist of caring about our children's emotional wellbeing.'

'Mavericks. Go back to work.' Silva laughed. She had unwrapped her cookie before the door was closed.

Eric let air out of his gritted teeth. 'Are you okay...with the baby thing?'

'Eric, I got knocked up in a toilet by what I thought was a stranger and kept it. It is only by happy accident – as per most of my life – that that worked out for me. I'm in no position to judge, and I'm happy for you.'

Eric nodded his head from side to side. 'Yeah, I'll give you that,' he grinned. 'Thank you. I know it must be weird that we're work buds and now I live with – and will be parenting with – your best friend.'

'Mate, you *are* one of my best friends. It's all good. It's nice to see you happy, man.' Silva said. 'Right. Hotel design brief. Are we almost finished with it?'

'Nearly. Let's have a look.'

Silva got home later that day, feeling accomplished. Their hotel designs looked great; each room having a nice chair to sit on, ideas for furniture and stockists, some of which they had found in Italy, beautiful but not cliché décor styles, and they were both very pleased with their work.

Rose ran up to her mother for a cuddle and Silva let her legs be hugged, lamenting being unable to pick her daughter up so she sat on the sofa and hugged her there.

'How was your day?' she asked Rose, who told her – in her own sensible nonsense – exactly what she had been up to. 'And what about Daddy's?' Silva asked. Rose budged up so he could sit down and stole a piece of toast off his plate.

'Oi! You're worse than the seagulls at the pier, you.' Jake

laughed.

'Well, the seagulls have the decency to only do it once. You have a lifetime of this little monkey.' Silva said. 'How was work?'

'Not bad. They asked about you. About my decision.'

'Did you tell them about Italy as well?'

'No. I don't think they would enjoy that.'

'Your bosses are awful.'

'Yes. But…they pay well.'

'Mmm.' Silva said, not wanting to stir the pot or influence him. She tried to relax her tongue and her jaw, the tension doing her no favours. Jake noticed.

'Did the hospital call you today?'

'No, why?'

'I thought they were meant to check in with you today. You look pale.'

'They haven't. I don't even remember that.' Silva said, suddenly feeling dizzy and tired as though Jake pointing it out gave her body permission to let go of itself.

'Oh…Dinner will be ready for Rose soon…are you okay?'

'No,' Silva said. 'I feel ill.'

Jake got up, dumped his plate and gently picked Rose up, letting Silva lay down on the sofa. 'I'm going to call the hospital. You rest a minute.'

Jake took Rose to the kitchen and called the labour ward. He set Rose free while he dished up her fish fingers and cut the heat out of them for her. The phone cut off without answering. He swore. He put Rose's dinner on her highchair table and rang again, checking Rose to make sure she was behaving. She was on the floor playing. Silva was asleep, her forehead hot.

Jake gave up on being answered and instead called 999. He described her symptoms and they told him to get her to the hospital within an hour.

He threw Rose's fish fingers and mash into a box, then somehow got Silva to wake up enough to get to the car, and Rose into her seat, where she could eat her dinner at Liv's, and then he sped to A&E, where he didn't dare breathe for the next few hours.

CHAPTER 20

'I guess it's decision time for your bosses then.' Silva said blearily, as she woke up in the A&E waiting room, took a sip of water, and gained some sense of real life.

'That's your concern right now? We technically have until our due date. But currently more concerned about you just kind of going limp mid-conversation.'

'Is Rose okay?' Silva asked, ignoring his concern.

'Fine. With my mum. The doctors should see us soon. They think you are in early labour, but they'll probably keep you here anyway owing to the weird start and high riskiness.'

'Silva Jones?' a scrubbed-up nurse called. Jake helped Silva up and they walked to the maternity ward. The nurse explained they had a bed set up ready and as soon as Silva was on the bed with her leggings off, a midwife had arrived and was checking her over.

'Looks like you've had a bit of a show. You're starting to dilate but you're not there yet. Blood pressure is still a bit high… we'll keep an eye on you in here for now. You might need some magnesium, you have preeclampsia, don't you?'

'Yes. Our midwife mentioned a caesarean?' Jake asked.

'It may not be necessary. We would prefer to avoid that. But be prepared.' she said and scuttled off elsewhere.

'Well. That's that then.' Jake said and shook his head.

'I'm too hot.' Silva said. Jake fanned her, then put a blanket over her a short while later when she was cold. Trying to make her comfortable became his mission, and it was impossible.

Silva slept a bit eventually, leaving Jake with his thoughts. He asked himself how he felt about living in Italy, or America, but truly the thoughts were just blurry and refused to stay still.

It was impossible to forget that he was about to see his second daughter's birth. Despite his unconventional entrance to parenthood, he had been excited about this.

How could I have missed this last time? He thought to himself. Silva woke up, was checked again.

'How many weeks is she?' The nurse asked Jake.

'Erm. Thirty-six, almost thirty-seven.' he said.

The nurse nodded. 'Okay. I don't think we will prolong her gestation, but I'll double-check with the ward consultant.'

The next few hours passed in a blur. The doctor arrived and declared Silva safe to attempt a natural birth. Jake ignored his rumbling stomach but eventually caved and left Silva to find something for them to eat. He brought her a mix of things but she declined all but a little bit of chocolate.

It wasn't long before Silva started to push, her hands gripping his like an iron vice. Jake was disconnected from the pain. It was he, Silva, the midwife and the sounds of labour. He had seen too much of Silva and suddenly a piercing wail cut through the pain and marked the arrival of their daughter. Grasping for life, her arms pulled and grabbed at the air around her, trying to swim through it to find a place warmer than mid-air in the gloved hands of a midwife.

'She's a wriggler!' the doctor laughed and cut the cord. She was laid next to Silva's breast and she fidgeted until she found her spot. She had no trouble feeding.

The midwife smiled warmly at them, and Silva sank back into the pillows.

'Hello, little one.' Silva whispered. 'You're so ready for this, aren't you?'

'What do you mean?' Jake asked.

'Rose was harder to get to feed. She was a bit more...bewildered by being born. Not the case here.' she said with a smile. She felt the familiar choking rush of emotions hit her and then she looked at Jake, whose face was serene with wonder, and down at their baby, who was beautiful and hungry. Jake had tears on his cheeks. After a few minutes, the baby got bored of feeding and scrabbled around like a blind badger cub.

Silva proffered their squirming ball of pink flesh to Jake. He grinned self-consciously as he looked at his daughter with tears in his eyes, his big man-hands making her seem even tinier. The baby settled on his warm chest in seconds and didn't move or cry, just stared with barely-open eyes for a few moments.

Their little baby seemed like a butterfly on a rock; something so fragile resting on something so strong.

Jake squeezed Silva's hand and felt a rush of love wash over him, covering her, and their baby. His heart ached for having not seen this the first time. *I'm here now*, he thought to himself. *And there are decisions that need to be made.*

CHAPTER 21

'Do you have a name for her?' asked the midwife, holding up her paperwork. Jake glanced at Silva. 'She gets the final say.' Jake said and grinned. 'If I pushed half a stone out of my pelvis, I would expect the same.'

'Daisy.' Silva said, and that was that. Beautiful and resilient, would grow despite the odds. It already suited her, Jake thought, in the same way that her sister was beautiful but hard work. He smiled to himself at that thought. The midwife took her for a couple of checks, leaving Jake and Silva feeling bereft. Jake made some phone calls with the good news to Olivia, Eric, and Layla while another nurse checked Silva over to make sure she was all right.

'She weighs six pounds four ounces. That's good. We'll keep you in just to make sure your blood pressure goes down. Would you like some toast?'

Silva nodded. Jake felt tempted to ask for some too but thought he may get told off. He still had plenty of food in his bag and different priorities, he reminded himself. He also hadn't just gone through an excruciating child eviction.

His stomach felt like overstretched dough anyway. He wasn't hungry, just confused. Feeling the need to be more than he was, which was ridiculous; he had been an active dad for months, but something about this, about seeing Silva so vulnerable, made him realise he had to step up. To finally stop his bosses snapping at his heels for a decision.

It was 3 a.m. He didn't need to do anything at that exact moment. Silva surrendered to sleep after her toast, and Daisy was curled up on his chest asleep. He didn't want to put her in her cot. Didn't ever want to let her go, if he could avoid it.

'I hate my job,' he whispered to his newborn daughter. 'I don't think I've ever told anyone that. Our secret. For now. But it pays well. I could do it forever if it meant all of you were safe and well.'

Daisy did a little stretch that made his heart melt. 'So what do I *want?*' he whispered, realising he hadn't really thought about that before. He had just catapulted into something that had snowballed into a career that he had sleep-walked into, with bosses that liked his attitude and his flexible, easy-going life that meant he was available for overtime and to send to different countries. The life that no longer suited him.

He looked at Silva. Both of them were free spirits, he thought. It had taken her to be knocked up and slowed down for them to see each other in the blur of their own hurricanes, and he was so grateful it had all happened. A series of accidents maybe, but they had been the best experiences of his life. It all made sense to him then.

'Silva is living her dream…maybe I can dream, too.' he whispered to Daisy.

'What's your dream?' Silva whispered back.

Jake had to stop himself letting out a real laugh of embarrassment. 'I didn't realise you were awake.'

'I wasn't. But I have to pee and I want to know what your dream is now. Are you still holding her?!'

'Yeah.'

'Cute.'

'Do you need a hand peeing?'

'I think I'll be fine, my love. Tell me about the dream when I come back?'

Jake let out a soft chuckle into the near-darkness and lit Silva's way to the loo with his phone light.

'So. The dream.' Silva said, stroking Daisy's soft downy hair and stopping when she stirred.

'Let's go to Italy, Silv. I hate my job. I think I want to do something with food – and where better to go and do that than

Italy? I can learn in a proper restaurant. Then come back here and maybe try and start something? And you can decorate it?'

Silva grinned. 'That's my Jake.' she said. 'I think I hear him in there, not corporate suit and boot Jake.'

'You aren't mad that I'm holding our newborn while I tell you I'm quitting my job to start a business?'

'Normal people would be. Not me. This sounds like it'll be really good for you and besides, all expenses paid in Italy, you can go wild. Maybe for the first time in a long time, babe.'
Jake grinned, feeling lighter than he had in years. Silva kissed him.

'Now, put her down and get some sleep, please.' she said as she climbed back into bed.

'Yes, ma'am.' Jake replied, standing up and gently putting Daisy down into her little bedside cot, realising as he did how stiff his whole body was.

A few hours later, Jake called his bosses to decline America and inform them he was on paternity leave. They were not happy, but they accepted his response. He knew they would not renew his contract in January, but that was fine. He would be in Italy.

CHAPTER 22

A few years later...

It was very warm outside and Rose was walking with her mummy and daddy to the park to play. Her daddy turned behind him to check the restaurant door was locked and Rose impatiently put her hand on the door to help him check. She put her hand over her own painted handprint. Daisy followed suit over her own print. The paint had faded a little bit and her hands were bigger now; Daisy's would fit in Rose's print. Rose was going to need a new set but as her mummy took her daddy's hand, she didn't feel like it was the right time to ask.

She stopped for a minute, looked at Daisy, who was running ahead, and took her moment. She was a bit scared, well not scared, but curious to ask, because she'd never asked before. But it was on the telly.

'Mummy, Daddy,' Rose began.

'Yes, Rose?' Daddy replied, reaching for her hand.

'On the telly last night they were saying their little boy was an accident. What did that mean? Am I an accident?'

Her mummy was looking at her daddy, and he was smiling at her in that way that always made her smile back. Rose wondered what she had said that was so funny.

'You were a total accident,' he said and Rose stared at him, wide-eyed.

'Was I?'

They reached the swings.

'We never saw you coming. But all the best things start by accident. And you are the happiest accident of all.' her Daddy said and pushed her on the swing.

Rose was up high, the cold wind and warm sun on her face and she smiled down at her funny daddy. She didn't know what he meant really but she knew it wasn't a bad thing to be an accident because he smiled his best just-for-her smile when he said it. She noticed her shoes were still blinking red lights even in the air.

'So, what does it mean?' she asked her daddy later, while they all ate dinner. She still couldn't quite get it out of her head, even though they were having her favourite, sausages and mash.

'You're growing up too fast,' her Daddy said and smiled. 'It means your Mummy and I didn't *plan* to have you, but when we did, we were very happy that you came along.'

Rose considered this. 'Was Daisy a happy accident, too?' she asked, and Daddy looked at Daisy, maybe hoping she wouldn't repeat it if he said it. She did that a lot.

'Daisy was more of a surprise, but we were just as happy about her.'
Rose let that sink in. She was an accident and Daisy wasn't. She *thought* that was good.

'When adults make mistakes and they turn out good they make them again on purpose.' Mummy said, and she was smiling. Rose nodded and shovelled a big bite of mashed potato into her mouth.

'You will understand one day,' her Mummy said. Everything was *always* "one day." The days seemed to take a long time to come, but she thought that was good.

'And what about La-La, Opal, and Eric's baby? Was *he* a happy accident?' Rose asked insistently. Her Daddy laughed.

'No, Rose. Toby was not a happy accident. Toby required some meticulous planning, La-La and Eric *made* him, like Mummy and I made you, but he is actually La-La, Eric, Auntie Opal *and* Uncle Bob's baby. They had a lot of hospital visits just to get him in La-La's tummy. They all look after him.'

'So he gets DOUBLE the Mummy and Daddy?'

'Yes, I suppose so.'

'That isn't fair.'

'That also means he has DOUBLE the eyes on him watching him when he's being sneaky.' her Mummy said.

'Okay, I like just having you two.' Rose said quickly. Her Mummy and Daddy laughed.

'Any more questions, Rose, or is it time for ice cream?'

Rose tapped her chin in contemplation, 'ice cream,' she said, 'like the one in our restaurant!'

'She's definitely yours!' her Mummy laughed.

'We established that,' her Daddy replied. 'Ice cream, coming up.'

They ate dessert together and Rose inhaled hers. That was *definitely* good.

ACKNOWLEDGEMENTS

When people say 'it takes a village to write a book', I always recoil a little bit. I want independence, not to need help, but I have learned writing this that it just doesn't work like that. Asking for help has led me here, with a book in your hand (or within your device screen) whereas otherwise I'd probably be tinkering with it for another few years, or have abandoned it altogether in one of my regular strops. So in that vein, thank you to those who read it and gave feedback in the last push: Gill Taylor, Kelly Peatling, Gretel Hallett, Lu Craker, Claire Chandler and Becky Scott (who runs an excellent inclusive dance class, Missfits Workout). You all helped it get to the last bit of the finish line that I thought would never come. Thank you also to Sue Rooney, who believed in it and encouraged me when it was but a scrappy first draft all those years ago, and to all my friends and family who asked after it and offered me support/encouragement/alcohol as necessary. Thank you to Vix for being my in-house cover illustrator and for our so-far 12 years of adventures together. May we always have a Disney trip to look forward to and chocolate in the fridge.

Love and thanks to all who bought this, read this, will review and/or recommend it, and to anyone holding this having seen or bought it in a charity shop. You have made my dreams come true by doing so, and so I wish you the most excellent of days.

BOOKS BY THIS AUTHOR

Soft As Sin

A Jar Of Fury: A Story Of Bullied Child To Strong Adult

Printed in Great Britain
by Amazon